Long Division

ANNE ROIPHE

SIMON AND SCHUSTER · NEW YORK

Published by Simon and Schuster
Rockefeller Center, 630 Fifth Avenue
New York, New York 10020

Manufactured in the United States of America

Long Division

WHAT I'M DOING in this car flying down these screaming highways is getting my tail to Juarez so I can legally rid myself of the crummy son-of-a-bitch who promised me a tomorrow like a yummy fruitcake and delivered instead wilted lettuce, rotted cucumber, a garbage of a life. I'm not going gently into this divorce, but yelling and kicking all the way with blood and skin under my fingernails and hate balled up inside like a gallstone fouling up my vital functions. There are millions of bitter ladies running in little circles around this continent, fearing the future, loathing the past and wondering, ironically or melodramatically, depending on their temperament, how it is they ever arrived flat on their faces in the mud. Most of them straighten up, paint the eyebrows a little darker, turn the wrinkles into a soulful expression and sally forth like sirens without a song to go again, a new man, new name, new address—impurity piled on impurity to clothe a naked life.

Not me. I'll find something really new, another way. I'll be again the free soaring bird of my first sexual moments—tied only to the limits of my imagination. I'll tunnel like a mole through the mountains and the plains of this artificially inseminated country till I find down under the ground, forgotten by this nation of non-spelunkers, a treasure, a constitution, a declaration of independence, a liberty bell cracked but ringing, and there I'll wait for a man to come and love me wild till I can give birth again to something or other that will find its name and save us all.

Messianic? It sounds like a crazy-lady's thought, but it's not. It's one of those cultural threads that appear woven into the fabric of the Moog mind. This one because I'm Jewish. I'm a Jewess. I'm only an American until they decide to move again—cremating, gassing, crating in box-cars, but even so—Yankee Doodle, Paul Revere, Johnny Appleseed, Paul Bunyan, Jesse James, they crash around too—shadows of simple times, like post cards I sent my grandmother from camp, remnants of a childhood spent imagining Hitler carried down Fifth Avenue crouched naked in a small cage, as crowds jeer and throw balls of tinfoil, never suspecting my own cruel thoughts were poor relations of his.

Onesies, twosies, threesies, foursies, Cherries in the Basket, Flipsies, Backsies. Sarah, my child, has been playing jacks in the back of this station wagon for the last two miles, ever since we left the Lincoln Tunnel and started on this sad journey to end the past, to put a foot in the mouth of the future, and to see America, an educational tour, while we're about it. The ball bounces, the jacks spill, their little points rat-tat-tatting on the floor—Sarah catches the ball, or misses, scrambling on dirty knees to gather the precious pieces of her game. She's perfecting her concentration in a skill that she will never use, never benefit from and never need—but the effort at improvement is grand, the intensity of her concentration so strong that I'm reminded of the Hail Mary's of my college friend, mumbled endlessly into long nights, that gave no certainty of absolution.

Sarah has barely spoken to me for weeks. I look at her face, searching for her anger, a reflection of mine, but I see only vacant eyes longing to return to the television. I lean out the window of our apartment emptied of her father's books, emptied of his clothes, I watch Sarah jumping rope. "Teddy Bear, Teddy Bear, turn around." "Mary, Mary, how does your garden grow." "One, two, three, four"—Later she colors in her map of the U.S.A., carefully printing the names of the capitals of the various states. She walks around me, politely, as if I were the headmistress of her school or a saleslady in a department store. Sarah, my darling, an ice age has come upon us, a leukemia of love, a blood thinning. Maybe the cure is in the South where the warm Mexican sun, the fast foreign sounds of the Spanish language, the earth covered with worms and crawling lizards and bugs-with-many-legs, will bring a thaw.

I want to get to Mexico to tell the judge I do alone for ever and ever, I will alone in sickness and health, and then, when that formality is done, I want to drive south like Ruth and weep and weep amid the alien corn till the angels of the Lord take pity and send the apocalypse without further delay.

Now I am trying to reach Hershey, Pennsylvania, so tomorrow Sarah can visit the chocolate factories. I drive down this New Jersey turnpike, not yet far enough away from the city to feel different, to feel the eyes of friends and acquaintances off my back. We've been on this road before, and so the landscape, with its farms and cows and then shopping centers looming suddenly, luring us with giant-sized pictures of ice cream cones dripping down rosy chins, does not yet give me the feeling of adventure, but soon. I will go dragon-slaying—bring back his bloody tongue tied to the roof of my station wagon—and win the hand of a new Prince. Now I have to find a place to sleep. E Z Drive-In signs flashing on the side of the highway tell me I am only five miles from a plastic ashtray in which to place my smouldering head, letting the night hours turn my single body to cinders.

Sarah, Sarah, my sweet and beautiful baby, what will you eat for dinner?—A Howard Johnson's hamburger, a chocolate malted and the 1001 flavors of ice cream floating together in the sea, turning to gray blobs of flotsam and jetsam before your unenthusiastic eyes, that hurry me to pay the check so we can return to the room and you can sit in peace before the television, casting blue light shadows on the fake leather chairs. I will sit with you, fingering the dusty venetian blinds, pulling aimlessly at the cord. Perhaps I will send a signal—someone may think I am rendezvousing with a fellow spy—an Asiatic counter-cover agent for the insurgent arch-incumbent government of the upwardly mobile, technologically backward, moon-struck guerillas.—The formula I will pass on to the enemy—if I can remember it—is . . . ? I can still smell the odor of the swamps across the river from the Manhattan of my youth. I thought as I entered the turnpike that the smells of chemical malfunctions came from my car—

my beautiful blue wagon. The separation papers gave me custody of the imitation-wood paneled love I had driven on so many excursions. For a moment I had thought the oils and carbon monoxide were mixing in the motor and would explode, leaving little bits and pieces of my skin and guts plastered on the asphalt like a curious skunk or a slow rabbit.

HERSHEY, PENNSYLVANIA, is a small town after all. In the early morning sun, the stores seem lined up like soldiers for inspection on clean-swept streets that stretch as far as the eye can see. Children play with Yo-Yos on the corner, and bicycles are parked by the drugstore. The American flag waves from the porch of the Arnold Hotel, and the yellow fire hydrants are surrounded by pansies, purples and pinks nestling close to the black earth. The streets have common names like Maple and Walnut and Beech, and the neat houses are curtained and geranium-potted in the rhythms of another era when there were no kids with long hair tied in ponytails mainlining heroin or passing little bottles of amphetamines behind the stoops or in the littered back alleys.

Sarah and I have breakfast in a coffee shop which is air-conditioned to prevent the flies that swarm outside in the summer heat from entering and enjoying the sugar donuts that rest on plastic plates on the counter. Sarah is counting the miles from New York to California. Her unwatching eyes are often turned to a division or multiplication problem that is done and re-done on some invisible blackboard. Muzak is piped into each booth of the coffee shop, and the waitress brings us syrup in little paper cups, sealed for sanitation like the jelly and the cream. We eat mechanically. Sarah reads the menu and counts the items offered and tries to figure all possible combinations.

I think of other breakfasts—the first night I slept out in Greenwich Village with a boy I had met at a party a few months earlier. In the morning he was embarrassed to be in bed with a stranger and took me to breakfast at Nedick's. I had a hot dog and regular coffee. He went to pay the check and disappeared into the crowd on the street. I finished my coffee as if nothing had happened. Had hardly anything happened? I had breakfast at the Dôme in Paris with a man I loved—a croissant, *un café filtre*, brilliant sunlight on the orange chairs. I remembered a cape, a beret, an American tourist with a camera. My love, my admiration, exploded like the thousand clouds of pigeons that settled in the Tuileries, pecking fiercely at the crumbs of stale bread thrown by little old ladies with beards, whose sacks seemed never to empty.

Mining towns to the west sent their fancy folk into Hershey to buy at the better stores that flanked the main street. I wanted to walk with the crowds. Sarah wanted to return to the motel after breakfast in order to watch the morning giveaway shows. I insisted she come with me to see the chocolate factories, to shop for bangles and things in the shiny places and to see what it would be like to own one of the large houses with a big porch along the side avenues.

I could move with Sarah anywhere. I could take her out

of Miss Lennitt's girls' school, and we could re-settle in Hershey, Pennsylvania, or anywhere else on the map that pleased me. New York was only the first stop, the disembarking point for my immigrant grandparents—why not move like the sediment in the bottle down to the bottom, or sideways, or crooked?—I could fly like a poisoned arrow in a hurricane and light most anywhere.—I dragged Sarah to look at the chocolate factory.

The industrial buildings were obviously the showplace—the real heart of the town. Signs pointed in the direction of the factory on nearly every street. The drugstore, the five-and-dime, all sold souvenirs—key rings, napkin rings, bookmarks, sweatshirts, etc., with pictures of large Hershey chocolate bars, neatly wrapped, the blocked silver letters promising sanitation and good quality. There were posters in all the storewindows—some showing old ladies in rocking chairs with half-eaten bars in their hands, others showing small children, their faces smeared with chocolate, holding up to the artist's eye a giant candy bar. I asked Sarah if she wanted to buy some chocolate in the nearest drugstore. "No, thanks, Mother," she said, her eyes calculating the distance from the center of town to the outer edge of small bungalows, used-car lots, Dairy Queens and drive-in movies we had passed on entering the night before.

We drove to the factory. The buildings were large, white-brick edifices with no windows. The gardens in front of the plant were blooming with roses, marigolds, peonies and hydrangea. A large WELCOME was written in the ground with smooth white stones. Public tours ran through the factory every hour. I wanted Sarah to see what industry was, what large machinery, droning, clanging and whirring, formed the background sounds to all the things we so easily used. I wanted her to know of what century and of what country she belonged. While we waited in the lobby, on chairs with cushions on which somebody had needleworked the Hershey insignia in maroon and silver, I read the pamphlets placed on coffee tables around the room. The factory, I learned, had been founded in 1894 by the Hershey who had used his mother's candy formula to transform the little town of Bucksay into his own villa, his company town, his universe. He had owned the big house on the hill—his chief executives lived in the smaller mansions clustered about, and the workers lived on the flatland, in the small but neat houses that formed the main sections of the town. The railroad stopped at the back of the factory and took away the cartons of wrapped chocolate, spreading the sweet from New Orleans to Seattle, the money returning to Mr. Hershey and his heirs, and now the public stockholders. The great-great-grandchildren watch the chocolate bars blanket the nation and sigh with satisfaction and pride in the technology of candymaking that has brought such profit and glory.

On the mantelpiece over the large fireplace in the main waiting room there was an extra large can of Hershey's chocolate syrup. I walked over to it and saw that there was attached to it a silver plaque which read: "Here are the remains of George Hershey, 1909–1949. Cremated according to his wishes." The receptionist kindly explained that George was the son of the original founder who had run away to Paris to become a painter, he had fallen into bad company, painted landscapes of the Pennsylvania hillsides which lacked verisimilitude because he was living in Montmartre and could not correctly recall the light or quality of his subject. Eventually Pernod and absinthe caused him to become ill. Finally his Oriental mistress wired his father to come take him home. By the time the broken-hearted old man reached the American hospital in Paris, George was able only to utter his last request—to be interred in a syrup can on the factory's property. The father forgave his son the many delinquent years and followed through on his last wish. So George rested in peace if not in privacy on the mantel. I told Sarah the story. She stopped the jacks game she was playing on the marble floor just long enough to listen to me. Then she continued to flip the jacks in the palm of her hand, explaining to me that this was the most important maneuver to master.

A girl in a little red-and-white-stripe pinafore came into the lobby. She was chewing gum, and her lips were painted in bright red. She held a silver tray on which sample chocolate bars, some with almonds, some without, were attractively arranged. She offered them to us and to the other families waiting. Sarah refused. But then through the door came a group of little, ragged children. They huddled in a corner.

When the girl passed them, one spoke up. "Here are the stamps."

"All right, all right," snapped the girl, her smile disappearing. She gave them each a bar and took stamps from them.

Then she explained to me, "We have a food stamp system here for children—they've found it's cheaper than a school-lunch program."

The door squeaked open; a little man crept into the room, furtively looking over his shoulder. The receptionist was busy on the telephone now, in a fierce hassle with her boyfriend over who had insulted whose mother the night before. The little man was wearing dark glasses and a windbreaker zippered up to his neck. He saw me staring at him and, much to my alarm, sidled over to my chair.

"Nice day, Ma'am," he said, tipping a porkpie hat with a jaunty little feather in it.

I smiled discouragingly, coolly, and returned to the pamphlet on company history that fluttered in my lap. The little man leaned over me; his breath smelled of a lifetime of pizza and grinders and submarines.

"Would you like a souvenir of your trip?—a dirty post card made right here for the nice people who come to visit? You look like a lady who would appreciate a little humor," he winked at me conspiratorily.

My mind filled with pictures of his friends, his colleagues, his predecessors, standing beneath the Arc de Triomphe, in the plaza near Chartres, in the corner café in St.-Germain-des-Prés, a weasel in front of the vesper store on the Via Veneto, a bat from a cave who peddled his pictures near the newspaper stand on Maximilianstrasse.

Here again in Hershey, Pa., I looked up, wondering for a moment if I was hallucinating. The other people in the room were watching us. Sarah had turned her head away from the man and was bent over the floor counting her jacks, but the receptionist had spotted him and was trying to terminate her conversation on the phone while waving to the gentleman to leave the room. An impulse never indulged in before came over me, and quickly, with the surreptitiousness of an experienced sinner, I plucked out a dollar, hard-earned by my soon-to-be ex-husband, and pressed it into the sweaty hand that reached out to grab it. He dropped into my lap a sealed envelope. I held it for a moment, imagining the fornicating couple I would see—the buxom local whore photographed while sucking or blowing or being sucked. I turned the images over in my mind, feeling a curiosity bordering on arousal. Self-disgust pushed me to end my own fantasies and open the envelope. There was a photograph, a close-up of a toilet. Inside the bowl I could make out the traditional floating objects. Across the top of the post card was printed "Hershey's chocolate makes your B.M. browner"—no lady fornicating, no whore selling her ripe flesh—only a toilet bowl like all the others I had seen since my diapers were first removed. I had been cheated, not a thing to brood over—just remembered so I would be wiser the next time.

The other families were staring at me peculiarly; a certain hostility was clear. I was the only parent alone with a child. All the others were in groups—four, five, three—made up of male and female and offspring. Like an unnatural mutation, I felt awkward in the normal universe. Like a pilloried adultress, or a stockaded petty thief, I felt exposed, my vulnerable pants pinned down.

I reread the publicity material in my lap and thought of that time in Rome when he and I had gone to hear the Pope at Easter. The crowds surged through the Vatican Square, mamas, papas, cripples, paraplegics, virgins and whores, all kneeling on the hard stone. His Holiness appeared on the balcony, and the crowd surged forward; a murmur, a prayer, a cry for help and mercy rose in the air. We stood to the side, pressed against an old stone wall. The Messiah has not yet come, I wanted to yell, fools and bastards, superstitious lunatics, I wanted to scream at the crowd. In Galileo's name I hate you all, murderers, crucifiers of a million Jewish children, a billion Turkish mothers, murderers of Buddhist monks, of gypsy dancers—and as I was listing the dead, the Pope suddenly was speaking, his frail arms hanging, waving like those of a broken bisque doll above the adoring crowd, and a flock of doves released from their cages flew above our heads—Ah, ah, ah, went the crowd. If God had sent a million doves to dance above the head of Job's wife, she would not have been consoled for the loss of her children. I felt like her, my sister of ancient times, Jewish and cursed—surely the next victim in God's metaphysical game in which I was not even a principal player, merely a prop on the stage set, to be broken so that the lead player could learn to weep.

At last a large gold-leafed clock chimed the hour, and a young man, dressed in a brown suit, came to take us on our tour of the premises. "This way, ladies and gentlemen"—and he pressed a button on the wall, and the large portrait of the senior Hershey swung away from the wall to open a passageway into the factory itself.

The factory was air-conditioned. The workers wore white uniforms. The floors were washed down by a machine every thirty minutes, we were told. The workers stood in lines near the belts that carried the completed bars in groups of twelve. The workers removed a tray and placed it in another machine, which made a retching sound, similar to that of my sheepdog friend's throwing up new grass he invariably ate. Out of the bottom of the machine came the wrapped candy. Occasionally one would be damaged; it would be thrown in a basket, taken away to be reprocessed later.

For twenty minutes we walked through the maze of tubes, pipes, presses and lines of quiet workers—quiet because the whir of the machinery, the grinding of gears, made conversation difficult. We finally came to the center of the factory. We walked up a ladder with handrails and little printed signs urging care at each step. We stood twenty feet above the large vats in which the beans, the milk, the sugar were boiling and cooking. We saw the funnels that poured the ingredients into the tanks below. It was a level of Hell Dante had not reached. It was very cold in the room, and Sarah kept her arms around her chest and hunched her delicate frame together to avoid the blasts of cold air that came out of the vents that cooled the hot pipes that fueled the giant vats. We walked along high above the ground. We were now deep in the bowels of the factory.

There was nothing to remind you of sunlight on leaves or other summer days spent at the beach. Still, my mind could not control the images of rosehips growing on leafy bushes by the dunes, long stretches of sand salted with the skeletons of sea life; the beach grass like a green velvet carpet, each blade blowing in the wind, undulating like the water to natural rhythms; the sea gulls, their wings spread, searching the sand with greedy eyes for an abandoned french fry, a hot dog half eaten, a small fish thrashing in shallow waters. We made our way carefully on thin catwalks now, going single file into the cooling section where the hot chocolate sat in tanks waiting to be funneled into the machine that would shape it into bars and send them to an upper floor of the factory where they would be wrapped and moved on their way. I had been at the beach just after we were married and I had turned as dark as a betel nut; and I had swum far out in the surf, daring the undertow to touch my charmed body. I had risen above every crashing wave and had controlled the sea. A strange odd tendency in a Jewish girl—we are ordinarily not athletic. We don't win golf tournaments or tennis meets, nor has a Jewish girl ever swum the English Channel to get to the other side. We don't seem to be represented on the teams that jump hurdles, do acrobatics, ski down mountains or run on tracks.

Just a generation or so removed from the sheitl that covered and bound a wife's head, a Jewish woman's hair does not fly free in the breeze, but is tied in kerchiefs, ribbons, rollers, hairspray. Our bodies move in small concentric circles, from stove to bed and back again, though the mind is free as it has always been to leap into dark chasms and run the everyday facts of life down the streets of an interior Pamplona where the festival of the bulls is an unceasing event.

Sarah leaned over the edge of the catwalk. She was counting the tanks of chocolate that lay below in brown thick pools. She couldn't clearly see the entire large floor because her view was blocked by interweaving pipes and ladders and by a crew of men in the usual white uniforms who seemed to stand around and watch the process—their function being unclear from the distance above. Suddenly a fat lady, who was on the tour with us with a whining little boy and a sunken-chested and no-chinned husband, pushed past me, saying, "Listen, my little boy has to go to the bathroom, let me through, let us out." The child held his penis through his pants and did look as agonized as anyone I've seen. The fat lady pushed me aside and jostled Sarah who was leaning over the rail, her feet in her new Mary Janes off the floor. I saw it happen, as if it was slow motion, as if I were too paralyzed to move, a nightmare of a second that seemed an eternity of dread anticipation. Sarah screamed as she fell. "Mommy," the voice called as it soared downward toward the chocolate below. I was still, as if I had fallen off a horse and could not get my blood or my brain to respond. Fear numbed me. I felt like the lifeless zombies of the early horror films I used to see Saturday afternoons under the starlit roof of a local Loew's.

I moved to the rail and looked over. I could see Sarah in one of the vats, kicking her legs and moving her arms in the best crawl she could do—she had become an Advanced Beginner Red Cross swimmer at the Mt. Pines Day Camp she had gone to last summer. Thank God she had not hit the edges of the tank or the floor. But could she move in the hardening sticky substance? I saw one of the men in white climb a ladder by the tank's side and strip off his shirt and pants, revealing a brown bathing suit with the Hershey insignia. He dove into the tank, bringing Sarah in a matter of seconds safely to the side. He helped her climb a ladder to the top of the vat and then to the floor. Our tour guide told everyone to be calm. This happened occasionally, he said, which is why life guards were posted by each of the tanks.

"Madam," he added, "you can reclaim your daughter at the end of the tour."

I wanted to rush to my child's side, reassure her, wipe the heavy chocolate from her eyelids and kiss the back of her thin neck, take her back to the E Z Drive-In Motel. Let her watch Dave Garroway, Newlyweds, and The Price Is Right, till her eyes fall out. Comfort her with *Mad* magazine and a promise never again to drag her away from the soft blue light of her familiar tube into the dangerous realities of the outside world. But the catwalks permitted no backward motion, and it seemed I had no choice but to proceed through the next area where the chocolate was poured into molds, and there listen to the guide tell his story with fake animation. The little boy who had had to go to the bathroom had wet his pants over the excitement about Sarah, and his mother kept glaring at me as if I was responsible for his lack of bladder control.

The guide told the story of the assembly-line worker who invented an improvement for the machinery and was given a one-week holiday, all expenses included, in Hawaii. He told of the historical time when the heating apparatus went wild and the chocolate burned and the almonds cracked, and they threw 1000 tons of hard bitter burnt chocolate into the Shenandoah River. Unfortunately the dumping concern allowed all the chocolate to be released in one spot, causing a flood in the area. Twenty-five houses and several people were lost within hours, but the place is now a lovely man-made lake called Hershey's Fancy on which the factory's executives and their families vacation in the warm months. At last the sights, the sounds, became familiar, and we were back where we had started; a large panel in the wall moved and swung open, and we were in a waiting room adjoining the one we had been in before. On the wall was a portrait of the second Mrs. Hershey, with a string of diamonds about her matronly neck and a little bouquet of violets held high in white-gloved hands.

"Sarah"—I looked around—"where may I find her?" I asked the tour guide, while tipping him as I had noticed everyone else doing.

"They'll bring her in here in a moment, Madam," he said, so I sat down and waited.

In a few moments the room was empty. I heard the great wall-door clang, meaning a new tour had started through the factory. I felt uneasy. A funny cold spread over my legs and thighs—Alex had always claimed I was breathing on him too hard, expected too much of each canvas, was driving him crazy with my respect—calling too many galleries, sending too many letters to museums; I was like an intravenous tube stuffing him with appreciation without his will or choice. But sometimes he would crawl over me at night, his head on my breast.—"Am I any good, will anyone care, am I a pretentious bastard, am I any good at all?"—and I would take his head in my hands and hold him as if I could protect him from the waves of emptiness that broke within, splashed over the dams of reason and flooded him with dread. At two or three in the morning I would make him lime Jello with bananas like his favorite nurse used to do, and we would sit on the floor together talking of travels we wanted to make to the Aegean or Morocco or Nairobi. If Sarah had hit her head on the chocolate vat, I would be totally alone. At last she appeared, led by a young girl in a candy-striped uniform. She had showered and was wearing a candy-striped skirt and shirt herself, but since they were so large, she looked ridiculous and very pale.

I rushed over to kiss her, to hold her in my ineffectual maternal arms. "I'm all right, Mother, I'm fine," she said, pushing me to a respectable distance. "Forty-two people fell into the vats over the last six years. That's an average of seven people a year." She was barefoot; her new Mary Janes dissolving in the vat would no doubt add delicate seasoning to someone's chocolate bar.

We went back to the motel. She assured me she had not

been frightened. Swimming was only a little difficult in chocolate. She did tell me she planned to write her father a description of the episode. It would give her something to say in the letter she had promised him.

"Did you think you were going to die?" I asked. "Did you have your eyes open or closed when you were falling? Did you think of anything or anyone?" I wondered if time at the edge of death was different—if it was slow and filled with memories, or blank and empty like a preshadowing of the future.

Sarah said, "Oh, Mother, let's forget it. I'm all right now." Her eyes were shut against my curiosity. She seemed to have none of her own. To have lived ten years, to have nearly died, and not to want to think about it seemed to me unbelievable. Sarah, Sarah, have you died already? Have I taught you to be too clean, too neat, do you ice-skate too well, play jacks (second best in your class, you tell me), jump rope, all with eyes that don't open, don't cry? Thank God nothing serious happened. I would have lost my last link to the everyday world, my responsibility for her care; her happiness anchors me, directs me on this globe so I am not blown apart like a puff ball—a dead dandelion in a light summer breeze.

Back in the motel, Sarah turned on the television, curled up on the nylon rug with a box of Mallomars I had bought. I lay down on the bed, remembering the white sand at the beach in St. Croix where the coconuts fell to the ground from the palm trees. The water was bright blue, and Alex and I had gone snorkeling, with masks, flippers and breathing pipes. We moved like awkward turtles over the surface, looking at the coral, the wide fans, the spread of sea plants growing in mysterious lumps about the ocean floor. We followed schools of little green fish, blue fish, shimmering with iridescent colors, darting in and out of the coral caves. We were intruders, our quietest movements causing alarm below. We were witnesses to the underwater universe, where the intricate eyes of the spiny catfish and the golden gills of the canary were part of the moving sea—a place that only intended death and decomposition for the human body. I stopped often, blew the water out of my nose, cleared my mask and looked at the shore that seemed always a little too far away. I followed his form in the water, his hands motioning me to follow. Suddenly his arm pointed straight down. There on the bottom, waving his long sharp tail, rested a sting ray, its flat gray shape not revealing where its eyes were set. We stared for a moment at the deadly form, and then slowly, as if we were tiptoeing away from the scene of a crime, we moved back to the shore, back to where the children were playing in the wild surf, where rafts and beach balls and suntan oil told of man's superiority to nature.

The soldier crabs spent the summer on the little hill above the beach. They lived for many weeks wandering happily in the woods; occasionally one would lose its way and crawl onto the sand. A little boy would tease it with a stick and bury it in a hole or hurl it back into the palm forest above the beach. The hard shell would knock against a rock or a tree trunk, and the sharp small pincers of the crab would flail out in primitive terror. Sometimes there were two or three in groups huddled on the sand, moving slowly toward the water's edge. A lady would scream as one appeared on her towel; another, terrified, found one, its claws out, its eyes hidden, its shell poised for battle, in her bathing cap.

We drank rum at the bar above the beach. We watched the rain come in ten-minute downfalls that drenched the hammocks, the patio; the great palms would swing toward the ground, their leaves heavy with rain water. Suddenly the hot tropical sun would reappear, the people return to the beach lugging wet towels and soggy sandwiches. The green water would return to blue and we would lie on the sand reading; our bodies touching, remembering the night. After a few weeks, we heard a rustling in the woods, a sound like rain or wind on the leaves, but there was nothing in the still air. We looked at the ground, and saw the low-lying plants moving. We heard the clicking and knocking of shells that we had learned to identify as soldier crabs marching. We were told their time had come. They were moving toward the water. All day we heard the rustle and the clicking as the little claws made their way down the hill, behind the beach, across the patio, down over the rocks, through the palm trees that bordered the white beach. By nightfall some dozens had reached the sand. The next morning, when we returned, the entire beach from end to end was covered with the moving shells. Crabs, millions of crabs formed a floor that seemed from the distance, solid.

As we moved closer, the sound became a roar on the shore. The knocking of shells, the clicking of claws, on stone, pebbles and other shells, became like the oom of oriental wisdom, a sound in which all others were absorbed. The soldier crabs hummed in mounds, covered the low-lying hammocks, the bar, the bar stools. The sand was gone. Wherever we looked we could see moving downward toward the ocean another army, and still another. The humans retreated. We went shopping in town for discount liquor, for souvenirs. In Christiansted and Frederiksted we looked for cheap cameras, cut-rate dishes, pursuing the tourist passion for goods at a saving that would prove the trip with all its interior dislocations was worthwhile after all.

Several days later we returned to the beach. We could see the sand again, the noise of the crabs was there still, but now the vast army, Cyrus's Billions, was turned around and was heading away from the sea back to the green leaves and black dirt of the hill beyond. Little clumps remained, slow ones, late ones. Injured in the hot sun, a dead crab or two sprawled out beside its useless shell. The others had moved back, propelled by some secret print in their minuscule genes, back away, up the dark sides of the hill. The mating, the loving, the spawning of the next generation of crabs, was done; nothing to do now—the energy spent, the great orgy over, the last participants leaving, going home to the black hills to knock or click in solitude for a while, and then to die, when the little ones in their soft new shells begin to move on the forest floor. We sat on a clear spot on the beach watching the retreating crabs in twos, threes, a single straggler. The sky was brilliant blue, close to our heads, pulled tight like a bandage on a wound. That summer Alex painted four canvases of lines, bright clear sharp lines that stretched the entire length of the canvas, taut like rubber bands, in primary colors against a background of black. The hibiscus and the morning-glory grew red and purple in irregular splashes of bright color before one of our rented-cottage windows. That was the summer we conceived Sarah, not planning a future, but not wanting to deny anything.

All through the night he would drink—a rum and fruit

punch mixture that cost only a few cents. I watched him pour the liquor in the never-empty glass, and I was so admiring of his extraordinary capacity. No one in the Upper Bronx, no one my grandfather knew, drank the hours away staring at the horizon with eyes that turned to watery red as the dawn wakened the insects and the birds to their deadly chase.

I couldn't drink very much without quickly falling asleep and waking hours later with an unpleasant sensation in my mouth as if my tongue were swollen and my head was pinched by a football helmet, but I liked to sit on our screen porch and watch him drink. "It's boring here," he'd say. "We'll never come back—it's a long summer to drink down," and he'd laugh because I'd be shocked, shocked he didn't want to stay forever in Eden. If I were Eve, naked in the woods, I could manage to avoid the forbidden fruit forever—provided, of course, the bugs didn't bite my bare skin, leaving me perpetually aching and sore—but if the bugs were not allowed to bite, then it wouldn't be Eden for them, would it?

In the early evening we would sit and watch for the green flash—natives promised us that sometimes at just the moment the sun touched the water, the sky turned bright green. It was supposed to happen in St. Croix because we were near the equator. We watched, Alex and I, night after night. Once in August I went into the kitchen to fetch some ice cubes, and I heard him scream. I rushed to the porch. "I saw it, I saw it—the sky was neon green—like artificial flowers—like juke boxes—it was really green." He stood up and walked about. I wished I had seen it too. "Maybe," he said, "it's only for artists, this goodnight flash of green. Would-be kindergarten teachers have to settle for more prosaic colors—like pink or blue." I was hurt—I looked each night for the sky to change for me, but it never did.

BY TWO in the afternoon we were back in the car. Sarah had changed into blue jeans and had rewashed her hair, removing the last vestiges of the chocolate that had clung in little patches to her scalp. The road seemed empty for a while. There were no other cars going or coming on the highway—was I the only one moving into new orbits?—was everyone else nicely screwed down in one place or another? We passed through thirty miles of farm country.

Time took on a strange quality, as if we had been moving forever, as if each minute were a year, and yet hours passed without a clear sense of progression; the inner clocks seemed all suspended, and only light and dark gave a sense of hour. For the rest, the hypnotic effect of the constant motion on the smooth road made me feel like a monkey in a capsule a billion miles above the earth. I felt unclear, as if I'd had a nightmare of seven years of famine that only lasted a second or two of dreaming time. It was hard to remember what it was like not to be driving.

The trees looked blue against a gray and darkening sky. A truck went by, a huge red van packed with lamp shades, so easy to manufacture out of synthetics, out of lamb's wool or paper or silk from a worm's entrails. A Greyhound bus loomed suddenly out of the back of the road right behind me, horn honking. It forced me off the highway. I went onto the shoulder in my panic to make sure it had enough room to pass. The bus was filled with people, its green belly stuffed with luggage. Where were they going? An advertising man from Rochester, New York, to visit his mother dying of hypertension in Abilene, a young girl headed for typing school in St. Louis, a salesman of Waring Blenders whose car had broken down in Harrisburg and had to get back to the home office in Cambridge? I pulled back onto the highway, thankful that there had been no steep embankment or sandy turf.

The sky got darker and darker, though it was still early in the afternoon. At last the rain came, heavy, with the pounding rush of a summer storm, the thunderclaps like giant farts directly above our heads. I pulled over, as the sheets of rain on the window made it impossible to see. The thunder seemed to shake the ground. I rolled up the windows so we wouldn't get wet, and we sat in the hot airless car watching the lightning flash in white sheets over the hills.

Sarah sat quietly in the back, her head resting on her arm. "Sarah," I asked, "are you afraid of the thunder?" When she was little she used to climb in my lap and bury her head against my shoulder, and we would count the seconds from lightning flash to thunderclap, listening for the storm to recede. Her head would get damp, and her hot hands would hold my neck, and I would fold my body around hers as if I were more than spit and dust and could actually protect her from the elements, the furies of nature. Now she had grown beyond sharing fear.

"No, no, I like thunder," she said. "Miss Nevins" (her

fourth grade teacher) "says the thunder is God's way of talking to sinners."

"Really," I said, "what did God have to say to Miss Nevins?"

"I don't know," said Sarah. "She didn't say," and we were silent listening to the heavy fall of the rain. I tried to turn on the radio, but the static with its ugly non-human cackle prevented any continuous sound from coming through.

Alex had painted the lightning and thunder once. The people who bought the canvas thought it was a painting of death. They have so willingly loaned it for exhibitions, group shows, retrospectives, charity affairs, that I suspect they really didn't want it in that special spot in their living room between the Rauschenberg they had bought when they first got married and the Utrillo their parents had given them for a wedding gift. I thought of it now—a black box, a rectangle in the middle of the canvas, and a straight gold line bisecting the work directly at its center. I was so in love with the pure form of the thing, so ecstatic at the fulfillment of a vision, that I didn't notice how cold he seemed to my touch, how his eyes looked away from mine into a room where other women walked; the swing and cut of their bodies, the size and position of their breasts, made them vases, vessels of other potters—and he was interested, always alerted to craftsmanship, and I sang songs of glory for the painting of the thunder. And at the party we had that night, he took a girl to bed, a mannikin like me only colored differently, and I could see when I reached out to hold him that like a palette muddled by too much mixing, by too much effort that brings about nothing, I was through.

It was hard to believe that the plastic that held us in relationship could find a solvent. I had thought that I was attached to him permanently like a barnacle to a mussel shell, but I was deluded. I was easily scraped off, I fell into murky waters. Alex had gone beyond his need for my reassurances, my particular body; now he craved adventure, variety, and he turned to women with high style, eyeshadow like butterfly wings, and jewelry made of old automobile spark plugs. Nearing thirty-eight, he didn't want to miss a single party in which a girl would be covered with whipped cream and someone allowed to lick her clean. I thought that since Sarah was now in school, maybe I should get my training in early childhood education and cut out large letters from construction paper and decorate some classroom with the rudiments of learning.

The painting of the storm hung for a while in the studio. A great symbol of the essence of thunder, the core beneath the motion and the sound, stripped of the heat of human reaction, the storm lay revealed, and often I avoided looking at it because of the weight of the black box that seemed to be crushing a field of wild flowers hidden unpainted beneath it.

I speeded up after the storm. I drove fast and sure, one arm hanging out the window, the other lightly at the wheel. Sarah read *Mad* magazine, laughing hard now and then at some hate humor that knifed the entire adult world directly in its collective liver. Often she didn't get the joke and would ask me to explain the cartoon. I tried, but my words hung heavy in the car, and finally she stopped asking me. The road was flat, through farm country—red barns squat on knolls in the distance, fat cows flicking their tails—browns, black and white Guernsey. Always they faced the same way as if turned to a cow-Mecca, praying for hot sun, cool grass and good bulls, while the cars on the highway flashed by like memories.

I stopped at a gas station, by the sign of a flying horse—a red Pegasus. A pimply-faced youth, a boy with a future that had to be drearier than his present (a face that revealed thoughts of pinching girls' bottoms and hopes that one might let him maybe suck on a tit on Saturday night in the back seat of his parents' car) came and lifted the fuel flap and inserted the hose in the back of the car. The image of childhood enemas prompted me to leave the car and take Sarah into the ladies' room on the side of the station. The smell was immediately overpowering. The plumbing was bad and the passing travelers messy. Toilet paper lay crumpled on the floor, lipstick-scarred tissue clogged the sink, a lidded can for sanitary napkins bulged and its contents overflowed—stale blood, rancid urine, and the scent of a bad deodorant or hairspray lingered in the bare room.

"I don't have to go," said Sarah. "I'll wait outside."

I couldn't blame her. I sat on the toilet, my bottom not touching; fear of germs, disease or even such intimate contact with strangers as a trace of sweat of a body on a toilet seat disgusted me. So lonely and horrified we are in little cubicles doing our necessary things for survival. Perhaps in a utopian world all the toilets will be in the center of the living room—public bathrooms will have no doors, and we will have bowel movements and talk with each other while watching group evacuations; no more lurking, sneaking around in powder rooms, pretending we are statues whose marble insides remain steady during centuries of hard wear. Maybe then the bathrooms will all be clean and beautiful, with vases of flowers on little shelves above the toilet paper. In orange lipstick on the mirror was written "Mary Jean remembers Joe." My God, poor Mary Jean with only memories to write about, a future bleak, a present vacant, a little girl with curlers in her hair, her man gone to bustier, lusher things—or maybe the army snatched him away. Their love had hardly ripened, and she in smelly toilets remembers what might have been.

Sarah had an orange crush from the machine by the station-office. She was playing jacks on the office floor when I came out of the bathroom. The pimple-faced youth was watching her, his mouth open—whether in wonder or lascivious attention, I wasn't quite sure. We got back to the car and on the road.

Four hundred and twenty miles to Springfield, Ohio, she told me. At fifty miles per hour, we should be there in six hours. Her voice was curiously flat.

"When we get further west, we'll see an Indian Reservation," I promised by way of encouragement.

Sarah wanted to go because she planned to buy presents at the reservation for her friends, but she said, "I don't like Indians."

"What do you mean?" I asked.

"Mary Ferguson said that her mother told her that Indians don't brush their teeth, or comb their hair or even take care of their personal parts." Sarah giggled a little at the intimate details she had almost but not quite mentioned.

"But Indians, Sarah," I started, "it was their country."

I went on a bit but I soon heard the rat-tat-tatting of the jacks and knew I had lost my audience. Don't you dream sometimes, Sarah, of being a little brave—running naked through a pine forest, putting your ear to the ground, hearing the faint steps of a deer or a bear, swimming in a cold hidden stream beneath the ferns and bushes rich with wild berries? Don't you think ever of sleeping at night in a buffalo skin, protected from the snow and the cold of a prairie winter? Will you ever feel guilt, Sarah, guilt for the genocide of a living people? One culture rides over another. The Hittites ravaged the Babylons, the Romans crushed the Greeks, the Assyrians destroyed the Medes, and the Greeks ran amok amid the ruins of Turkey, and the Americans came, and each one destroys a little more, builds on the ground that had before been free, and the guilt remains, causing blindness, madness, birth defects, immunity to vaccination, no remedy yet found, each civilization carries in its guts guilt that gives birth to more guilt, that like a cancer spreads to vital parts causing strange convulsions.

Up ahead were hitchhikers. I had been warned in my prim youth never to pick up hitchhikers; murderers, rapists, sex perverts, wait on the side of the road for soft-hearted ladies to slow their cars. Then at knife point force them into back roads; unspeakable acts, products of disease and cruelty, are easily done. But I saw three young men with long hair, patched blue jeans, a guitar—youth culture, love culture—seeing the country. Who in Ohio would help them if I left them behind? I slowed the car and stopped.

"Why are you picking *them* up, Mother?" Sarah whined at me.

"Because," I said, "we are all brothers."

"Oh, Mother," she said in disgust. Already she knows a cliché, a deceit, an adult lie to cover an impulse, to moralize over my need for diversion from the gray boredom that was stretching within me down the longest road I had ever known.

I stopped, Sarah was thrown forward, our suitcases banged against the sides, the brakes squealed. The boys smiled. I saw just some gold in the back of his raw gums. His few teeth were yellow and stained—a counter-culture revolt against the toothbrush, the routine, the methodology, the Babbitlike mentality it takes to buy, carry and use the nylon plastic brush regularly. The result, toothless freedom.

"How do, Madam," said the one with the long blond curls that hung down his back.

Troubadours, poets, artists of a new life, my sympathy was with them. I was too old and too rigid to put a knapsack on my back and run with the children on trips, to travel in the brain or on the road. I could only admire the style—the soul of the Hansels and Gretels that wander through the forest, the breadcrumbs they leave behind eaten by fierce birds, the dark night always closing in.

"We're on the road, ma'am, headed for our camp outside Springfield. We've got a big meeting tonight, the brothers and sisters from five states are gathering."

"What kind of meeting?" I asked.

"Oh, a place," the little one with barely a beard said, "a place to let the Lord shine in, to let Jesus walk among the brethren and for us to touch the hem of His robe in the place that was made for Him on this earth." He was practicing to be a preacher, warming up on me for the bigger audiences he would one day face.

The third one handed me a red card with a pink flower

painted in magic marker. On each petal it said in bold print, "Jesus Saves."

I had not picked up three bohemians, three representatives of the American youth, of the greening revolution, but three antediluvian throwbacks, three disciples of a dead principle. The creators of great churches, great powers, Bishops fat with ermine robes and emerald rings, had always been preceded by these same fanatics, believers who went among the people in blue jeans and sackcloth—my enemies are everywhere.

"I'm hungry," said Sarah.

Before I could answer, the tall curls said, "Whatever I have, I share—it is yours." He took from his pocket a roll of mint Lifesavers and offered them to Sarah.

"Thank you very much," she said. The little preacher took out of his knapsack a comic book. "Oh, 'Horrors of the Dungeon,'" Sarah squealed. "That must be good." The little preacher didn't share his comic but started to read.

The curls said to Sarah, "Are you and your nice mommy with Jesus?"

"Well," said Sarah, "I'm half Jewish, and in New York City where I come from we don't really talk about that sort of thing. Do you have another comic in your knapsack?" She smiled her sweetest at him.

The preacher-boy reached in and handed her a well-thumbed copy of "Ghoul's Paradise." "Jesus is for everybody—no prejudice against race or creed, ma'am."

"Glad to hear it," I said, feeling grim. A curiosity pushed me on. "How long you three boys been interested in religion?"

"Well," said curls, "I've been into this Jesus thing three

years now. My daddy is a dentist in St. Louis, and we've never been particular church people. We have a country house in the lakes area and in the summer me and my friends would do a lot of motorboating. There's not much about a Chris-Craft motor I don't know. But then, you see, I didn't want to go to college. My daddy kept talking about oral surgery. I couldn't see all those years shut up in school, and then a lifetime of looking down gullets. I got asthma, and my mother saved all the doctors' letters and bills from the time I was five years old so I could one day show them to the draft board, and I did and they said buddy you're free so I thought I'd just see the country doing jobs here and there. For a while I took a lot of what everybody offered, you know what I mean, lady, hash, speed. The works. But then I was out one night in a field outside Los Angeles—listening to those cars go by on the freeway. Zip, zip, like what's it all about, I thought. Zip, zip, like a giant anteater's tongue was snapping out and zipping all those cars, zip into his mouth. When I left home, my mother was needlepointing a cushion for the big armchair in our living room. It looked like it would be a pretty thing, but it was taking her so long, and she spent her nights with the thread and the canvas, in and out of those little holes. I thought, who for? I just couldn't see it and I got scared. Later this girl I met in a diner, she had a job driving a taxi, she turned me on to Jesus, and am I ever saved! I just do my time on this good earth, we thank the Lord every day, and wait for the Judgment time to come. Yes, brothers. Yes, Jesus. What's your name, lady?"

"Emily, Emily Brimberg Johnson."

The middle boy picked a few chords on his guitar, and

sang in a sweet gentle voice, "Emily, Emily, Emily Brimberg Johnson," though his breath that I felt hot on my neck smelled of onions and cheeseburger and tooth decay. "Three is for the Wise Men, Two is for Mary and Joseph, One is for the Lord God alone." Sarah leaned over to listen to him play. "Sing with me," he said to her. She looked embarrassed. "Jesus wants to hear your voice, and yours, too, Ma'am," he said.

Listen, I thought, I'm giving you a lift in my car, I'm not going to sing besides, don't push me around and don't let your Jesus do any pushing, either. He may be floating pale and bloodstained, his white robe billowing in the Ohio sky, rising and falling with the gentle wind above our heads, looking down on his children riding about on U.S. 40—and then again the sky may be empty of all but chemical collisions, molecules, nuclear fission, gases—a space without personality, a conception without a hard edge—no crown of thorns piercing the sweet brow, no salvation, nothing but a black empty hole where the corpses, now disintegrated, had once been.

Sarah had started singing "One for the Little Baby." I asked the preacher-boy if his parents were religious. "God, no!" he was quick to answer. "My daddy teaches driver education in Winnetka, Illinois. He thinks I'm crazy, but I forgive him, he can't help his prejudices. I send him pamphlets, show him the true word every chance I get. I sent him a big poster just last week, with Jesus and the people singing together in a giant rockfest. Real beautiful poster, it was nearly lifesize, too." Sarah was singing louder. She seemed to enjoy it, her hands were clapping in rhythm. "That's it, little sister, find Jesus with me, we're getting there."

No God for Sarah, no religion for the child of an Episcopalian painter and a Jewish renegade from a High-Holiday worshipping family. I had intended her to be the child of the future, the gold at the bottom of the melting pot.

"Two for Mary and Joseph, Three for the Wise Men bearing gifts, halle, halle, hallelujah."

Sarah said, "Sing more." There was a sweet virgin tone in her voice—innocence combined with ignorance made for a purity of the best kind.

I thought of the grieving bewildered parents; who at the time they held this little boy sweet at the breast and paid monthly dues for college layaway savings plans would have thought he'd end up tramping the road for Jesus? The third one had closed his eyes, nodding his head as the car hit a rise in the highway.

"What about your friend, when did he find Jesus?"

"Oh, well, he's still searching, but he's coming to the meeting with us, maybe tonight will be his night to let the Lord illuminate, clean out the dark corners where the devil sits and heats his irons, sharpening his spears for a return match with Jehovah."

I interrupted, "You mean he doesn't believe in Jesus?"

"No, no, he believes sometimes. Sometimes he goes back on the hard white stuff, and then he doesn't care any more, and sometimes he says he only believes in Krishna and the rest of us are pagan worshippers of a primitive religion. He stays up at night saying his hare krishnas, and then sometimes in the morning the good Lord brings him back to his senses, and he says he sees Jesus walking beside him, holding out His hand, telling him the hard stuff's okay—it's God's own gift to the little baby in the manger, and Jesus shared His white powder with all the other manchildren in the globe. My personal opinion is he's not got Jesus yet, but the Lord works in mysterious ways—maybe tonight, you'll bring him luck, and his head will get together, and on a wide meadow in the brain, Jesus will rise like a stalk of corn and His son will fall at His feet in true salvation."

"It's been a long time since I had any good corn on the cob," said curls, picking at his guitar, and we were all quiet for a while.

The road stretched on past a factory painted blue and white, its chimney billowing a green smoke in the pale Ohio sky. A large blue and white sign told us Ortho products, contraceptive jellies and creams, were the local produce.

From the valleys outside Cambridge, Ohio, at a steady 60 mph I moved further into the midwest, away from the harbor town of New York, into the heartlands where no smell of the sea could follow, into the great bowel of the countrytisofthee, and Sarah hummed along with the guitar "Swing Low, Sweet Chariot." The new slaves were again singing, having given up any hope for this vale of tears—"coming for to carry me home." Sarah smiled easy at curls.

"Come with us tonight," said the preacher boy. "You could drive us right up to the campsite and meet all our friends. The brothers and the sisters have sleeping bags all over this great field, and we got a big tent for the meeting, and we're going to have popcorn and cotton candy given out free to all the nice people who come to the meeting place."

Sarah started to play jacks again. Rat, tat, tat. The ball

bounced on the sleeping one's face. He didn't react. The preacher retrieved it for her.

"God gave you a gift with your hands, I can see that," he said.

"Well, Joan Carling is better than I am, but I'm second best in my class." Sarah stared out the window, her eyes closed, focusing on a jacks championship, or maybe, without my knowing it, her mind wandered past her present interests to a moment when she would have full breasts and a mound of pubic hair, and she would lie down before some boy, in total terror; like the maidens the Aztecs pushed off a cliff each year to honor their irascible god, someday she will stand at the edge of the mystery. Oh, my darling, I remember how you vomited for hours the night before you started first grade.

The road was flat and straight, bisecting the empty land into two irreconcilable halves. The late afternoon sun gave each telephone pole, the occasional farmhouse, the large chicken coop, the automobile graveyard, a distinct glow as in an El Greco painting. I sensed flagellants circling around somewhere beyond the ring of the horizon, whipping the skin off their backs, bloody and raw with chains of iron intertwined with thorns. I thought of the motel we had reservations at in Springfield: the restaurant with wilting flowers in plastic cups on each table, the waitresses with glazed eyes, behind which the highlights of last night's drive-in movie replayed.

"All right," I said to the boys, "we'll take you to your camp and come to your meeting."

"You're cool, lady. For an old lady you're really cool. Let's go."

WE ARRIVED toward sundown. Signs had appeared fifty miles back on the highway, Jesus ⟶ it said at Exit 12 on U.S. 19. Jesus ⟶ it said on the gas station, and so directly we drove to the large field someone had hired for the meeting. Cars were parked everywhere, not lined up neatly as at a football game, but driven randomly about, stopping at will in the clover. People were eating sandwiches, drinking beer and Coke, and lying on the rooftops of their cars watching the sky, possibly waiting for important appearances. A large red truck was decked out in psychedelic colors, and it had a little awning in stripes, and signs that said *Eat to Meet the Lord—submarines, pizza, soda with/without onion, mustard, lettuce, tomato, relish, catsup, etc.* The sleeping boy in our car had slumped over when curls and preacher got out, and there he lay, his face ghostly pale, still pock-marked from a long adolescence. His eyelashes were sparse and his blue jeans jacket had the world LOVE smeared in red paint across one breast.

"Is he all right?" I asked curls.

"The corporal form has only transitory meaning," he replied, disappearing into a crowd where he seemed to be known—at least he was instantly absorbed, the way an amoeba surrounds and incorporates a food particle.

Sarah allowed me to hold her hand as we made our way to the sandwich truck through the circles of young people sitting on the grass. I looked at the sea of youth and thought of the travelogues I used to see before the main feature started at my local Loew's: a mass of penguins sitting on slopes of ice in the Antarctic, blinking at the approaching cameras, flapping their useless wings and soon turning clumsily away; a horde of silly birds, heavy-footed, swaying from side to side, hurrying from the invasion of men to the safety of the cold sea. We picked our way over sandaled feet, bare feet, sprawled arms, babies nursing, men with no shirts, a group of girls playing with a ouija board. I thought of Alex on a platform in his studio, painting high on a ladder, a solid dark brown color moving across the high canvas. Under the ground, he said. Twenty feet under, this is the way it is, not what a miner sees trapped by an explosion, not little bits of silver reflected in the black hole with space already gray and black with dust and human breath, but brown is what you would see under the ground. Landscape, he called it. I knew after I saw the painting that under his ground no roots were pushing upwards, carrying the buds of future beets or hopeful stringbeans; no worms were meandering down, altering the density and quality of the darkness, no bugs hid in safety from the sharp beaks of the birds, no treasure of stones or pottery revealed the age of earth or spoke of civilizations long buried and forgotten. He saw a solid brown beneath the ground as if a metal band pressed hard against his eyeballs. The museum people loved it and squabbled among each other as to who would make the offer for it, and in whose books the reproductions might appear.

The day the first museum man came to the studio we were excited, but we had learned enough to wait for certain news. He borrowed six paintings and some photographs; two other associates and a secretary came the next week looking around. Three weeks afterwards the letter arrived in the mail. "We would be pleased to purchase, etc. . . ." We hugged, we kissed, we ran from the apartment down Madison Avenue. It was March and our coats flapped about us like wings of terror-struck birds. Everything would be ours—success, fortune and eternal happiness. It seemed as if we owned the city. Young and powerful, fame would bring a court, money, travel to little museums in Italy, in Greece. We didn't have to face the gray days of boredom because each week we could change our location, meet new people, and the success would inflate us above the perils of life. Like balloons we would float on a euphoria of admiration—There go Alex Johnson and his interesting wife up in the clouds again to have lunch with the North Wind and take a ride on the back of a monsoon. . . . But the next day Alex was strangely quiet. "Am I really good, you think? How do I know this guy is not full of it?" "Of course you're good." I hardly paid attention. "I'm used to the idea of fame now," he said. "I need something else." "What, what do you need?" I asked, feeling a crackling inside, as if my body were made of strudel paste. "I need," he said, "something better than a wife with just two breasts like every other broad around—I need something great." And with that he left for the night to roam the city, plucking what he could from the streets, drinking, and I sat in bed like a clam with a crushed shell, I oozed onto the sheets a little death.

All around me I saw young men and women in white T-shirts that were emblazoned with purple letters, "Go, go, go all the way with God." Six young girls were sitting in a circle clapping hands. "Two, four, six, eight, who do we appreciate? Jesus, Jesus, yes, yes, yes." Sarah was getting excited and beginning to jump up and down. She seemed more interested, more animated than she had been for a long time. She dragged at my sleeve. "I need a bathroom now." I looked over the mass of heads. I looked at the cars in the immense field so scattered, so many people. There would be no private place to squat. At last I saw lines of people standing before what looked like gray freight cars. I could see doors opening and closing as the occupants gave their places to the next in line. I recognized the portable bathrooms from demonstrations, long marches, and other public moments. I had always been a political shadow following the good people here and there. Alex always laughed at my drawerful of buttons, my good intentions. He claimed I was always collecting losers like some ladies collect jewelry. It made me angry each time he repeated this crack, but he had a certain point—my heroes were always virtuous but defeated or killed. Alex thought painting was the only subject worthy of words and few words at that; the more he drank, the more silent he became, till at night he would sit with a bottle in his studio listening to records while I sat with Sarah watching TV, wondering if I would have been a good teacher.—Perhaps I would have been a better nurse, but my grandmother thought it was disgusting to change bedpans, and the faces she made at the smells and sights she imagined I would experience convinced me to give up all desires for a nursing career.

We made our way over, across the limbs that sprawled about in the grass. I felt for a second as if I was on the set of a movie, a battle scene in which Custer had come down from the hills and killed all the flower children camped in the valley below. Any moment the director will call: "All right, cast of millions, play dead!"

"Power to the Lord!" "Right on for Jesus!" read the signs on the cups that mendicant teenagers passed about the crowd. Some organization, some bureaucracy, had paid the bills for this meeting, and the tithe must be collected. I dropped a dollar as a cup passed me by.

After a long wait for the bathroom, a long wait for a soggy submarine sandwich and a Coke, I went back to the car with Sarah. She climbed up on the roof to view the bodies lying on blankets all around, the way the seaweed had collected on the bottom of the boat we bought with the first sale of the blue and white triangle paintings. We sailed often the first summer; sometimes when we were becalmed I would lie down on the bottom of the boat and he would crawl on top of me and we would rock so hard I would be black and blue in the morning. I was so proud to have married an artist, as if his choice of me (it wasn't really a choice, I hung around him so long he finally got used to me) made me a kind of muse, a spirit freed from walking forever in the shadows of the elevated subway. I became an assistant visionary, so to speak. I didn't mind so much at first that he always looked and took other women—I thought it was sophisticated, bohemian, the way artists were supposed to be. As long as I remained devoted, muted and dull like a familiar couch or a worn chair, I thought he would always return home. When, finally, I started throwing things around the apartment so he would notice, he was offended at the noise and left. The following spring when we went to look at the boat, the barnacles had encrusted the bottom—thousands of small shells, a blight that would not easily yield to knife or hammer.

I looked in the car and was relieved to see that the sleeping one was no longer there. I took my cigarettes out of my purse and was searching for my matches when a pale hand tapped me on the shoulder. "Jesus makes tobacco unnecessary. Let the Lord come in. Let him breathe in your lungs! You won't feel tense, anxious, like nibbling or sucking on anything. Jesus saves, and you can throw your cigarettes away." With that he snatched my pack of Marlboros and threw them out into the field of people. He then, stoop-shouldered, tattered, touched by God, left me for other crusades. I looked in my bag for another pack, couldn't find it and so stumbled toward the place where I had seen the red and white package fall.

"Excuse me," I interrupted a group humming "Silent Night." "Did you see a pack of cigarettes that somebody threw right about here?"

No one looked up. I rummaged around the knapsacks, bags of potato chips and cans of cola that had grown like mounds of primitive graves near each group. I felt flustered, irritated and alone, cold and cranky. I thought it was a mistake, we should have gone to the Daisy Motel in Springfield, and I could have picked up a mystery in the local drugstore and lain in a clean bed, smoking all I wanted without any voices from God bullying me.

A boy in a black leather jacket stood up and came over to me. He had a silver cross hanging on his bare chest and black boots with silver spurs. His long dark hair hung down his back like crocodile scales. "Hey, lady," he whispered, "you want a souvenir of this remarkable occasion?"

"Have you got a cigarette?" I asked.

He pulled a pack out of his jacket pocket, and as I saw it, I felt a surge of relief, a return of my generosity; my appetite for adventure reappeared.

"Listen, lady, I have something for you to remember today by that will really blow your mind."

"What?" I asked, stalling, wondering if I dare ask for another cigarette to have for later.

"A porno Easter Egg! A really out of sight Easter Egg!"

"What?" I knew that it had to be a con game, a bad sell, a shill from 42nd Street in costume in Ohio looking for suckers. The first city apartment we had in the West 90's we watched the game every night. The guy would leave his apartment opposite ours on the fourth floor of this walkup and go down to Times Square. A while later he would return with a young red-faced soldier from the sticks. He would say, "My sister's in there waiting for you all undressed in the back bedroom. You give me your camera and your wallet to hold, and I will wait here till you are through, Amigo." The soldier, whose Boy Scout leader had taught him fifteen kinds of knots, gave over his valuables and entered the empty apartment. When, ten minutes later, he emerged puzzled and bewildered, afraid in his panic he had not seen the waiting girl, his newfound friend, his wallet and camera were gone.

A porno egg. I knew better, but despite myself images came: Mary Magdalene before reform, warming Jesus' balls; Joseph trying to get in; John the Baptist's penis erect on a silver tray, soul-kissing Salome. I knew I had to have at least a look.

"How much?"

"Five dollars," he said.

"All right, if I get your pack of cigarettes, too."

"Okay, lady, you're the boss," he said, dropping a pack of cigarettes he pulled from his jeans into my pocketbook.

I paid, and from a pocket inside his jacket he pulled a large sugar egg with the traditional sugar frosting, pink decorations and a little celluloid see-through window. I took the egg and wrapped it in my scarf and returned to the car. Sarah was now sitting on the grass watching a spontaneous modern dance performance by a skinny girl with hairy legs. I ducked into the front seat of the car and surreptitiously unwrapped my porno egg. I picked it up gently and, squinting my eyes, looked in. There I saw in a cottage setting a little cardboard lady bunny sitting on a rocking chair knitting a pair of baby socks. A male bunny, identified by a blue bow tie, was standing close. Around her feet were a dozen baby bunnies playing with toys, fighting, eating, etc. A caption written on a strip of paper like the message in a fortune cooky hung about the male bunny's head. It read: "Darling, you forgot to take the Pill again." I felt crushed. I had wanted at least a huge penis suspended from the cross. I reached into my purse for the pack of cigarettes. The second I lifted them up I knew I'd been truly and completely had. It was of course an empty box.

Ruth amid the alien corn, Sarah forever waiting for a reprieve from God that came only when she was unable to bend to kiss her baby, to follow his first steps about the house, incontinent, senile, beyond mothering; God in His cruelty allowed her to conceive and birth the baby from whom came the Jews, a tribe of misfits always out of step, the wisdom, sadness and incompetence of Sarah's old age, the unlovedness of Isaac written onto the genetic patterns of the babies to come.

The lights in the tent suddenly went on. I had not realized that it had grown darker; and fireflies, small lights, darted over the meadow between the moving heads and hands of the people, who, seeing the tent illuminated, gathered their belongings and, carrying cushions and blankets, moved forward. I found a sweater in the top of a suitcase for Sarah, and holding her hand, followed the crowd.

"Daddy doesn't believe in Jesus, does he, Mommy?" Sarah asked casually.

"No," I said. "I don't suppose. Painters, you know, are special, they don't need other people's words or images to get them to the heart of the mystery, the center of the universe." I wanted to tell her more, to explain the extraordinary fact of her father, but I couldn't find the words.

"Well, I'm not a painter," said Sarah, who indeed had shown no particular early gifts, although I had half expected the inheritance to reveal itself and had supplied endless boxes of crayons and reams of clean white sheets of paper.

We had reached the tent and sat down. The continuous hum of electronic equipment played havoc with my nervous system. Mikes boomed, joining sounds of fingers tapping, and voices were magnified to the decibel level of thunder. On the raised platform I could see a simple cross painted on a bedsheet suspended from poles, and then thousands of dollars' worth of equipment connected the gaggle of musical instruments to a battery-operated generator on the side of the stage. Flies atracted by the lights on the tent top flew above our heads, a moth or two lifted its wings with an easy grace.

The star preacher stepped forward: "My people, my dear people, here to let the Lord into your souls—Save, save for the next world. Cast out thoughts of this mean and evil ground, and turn your eyes heavenward toward the Father of us all and the Son who died that we may be redeemed." And on and on his words tumbled—the crowd was spellbound by his melodic voice, by the intensity and sincerity with which he delivered his lines, and beauty of his simple young face, his blond hair flying about like a nimbus, a sign of God. I floated on his words, a habit of a lifetime.

"Hic, haec, hoc, huius, huius, huius." The words hung over my head as I sat stunned and stupid like a pillar of salt on the desert, while the Latin teacher droned declensions of a dead language, a ceremony of letters, a ritual of what had been and meant nothing to me but exclusion from another magical circle. "Arma virumque cano, Troiae qui primus ab oris . . ." "I sing of arms and the man who came from the shores of Troy"—a great battle, a convulsion, a civilization dead and another born, a queen on a funeral pyre dead of love, and bodies strewn across the Mediterranean—responsibility laid at the feet of power, greed and lust. Dido—dear Dido—how stupid to die for a man who leaves you! What a disease to be so consumed with love and longing that you burn yourself up. Find another interest—teach Carthaginian children algebra, or roll bandages for the war-wounded; take a job, go overseas, don't burn in sorrow. Another ship may bring a handsome stranger. Pull yourself together, take up skiing or sailing or politics. Aeneas is not so special as you think. Burn the boots he left in your closet or the shirt he wore to the baths, but spare yourself—take up needlepoint, redo the palace, learn gardening, get new household gods. . . . I remember Aeneas carried his household gods with him wherever he went. "Lares and Penates." Mine are smashed. Centuries ago some stern ancestor struck down our idols. "Thou shalt not worship the graven image." Why? Why is it better to worship history and the words of dead men read over and over through the seasons of the year? Why is it not right to take a household god to bed, to cradle its head, stroke its stone or wood form, and beg it for just a little safety or a little peace?

The rock groups took over the stage, singing at the top of their electronic lungs, "Jesus, hold me in your lap, I ain't got nothing else to say, Jesus, Jesus, show me the way. This life just one bum rap. Jesus, Jesus, hold me in your lap." The words seemed flat, but the music rolled around inside my gut. My arms swung, my legs moved. I looked at Sarah—her eyes shone, she was alive. It stopped. Sarah sat down next to me, allowing her hand to touch mine. I looked at all the faces, pale in the glare of the electric bulbs, perspiring from the June heat and the music pulling them toward a vision—someone had already died for them, they wouldn't have to do it themselves—they could go on forever, salvation was as natural as responding to the music, as easy as turning on the radio. Another group came and sang in softer tones, "How many hours on the cross, My Lord, how many years to go?" They sang louder, something about a dog that drowned in the river Jordan, but I couldn't understand most of the lyrics.

Then the preacher stood up. "Take hands," he said in a great voice. Everyone stood up. "Take hands and pray. Pray the Lord will come into this humble place and take you and you and you and save us all tonight."

The drums rolled, the guitars hit a single high note, a trumpet blared, a hand grabbed mine. It belonged to a boy with dyed orange hair, puffy lips and a tulip painted on his sweatshirt that had once, many washings ago, said "Calvin Coolidge High." Sarah took the hand of a pregnant girl with long unbrushed hair. We stood in silence. Someone started humming "Nearer My God to Thee," and others followed.

There was a shriek. "I seen Him. I seen Him. I seen the Lord." And a girl ran forward crying, and laughing.

The preacher helped her onto the platform. She was too overcome to tell us her own story, so the preacher announced, "The sister has been saved. Thank the Lord."

A shill, I wondered, an actress, or had she seen God Himself in purple robes, sitting among her friends in this meadow in Cambridge, Ohio? Had He said to her, "Ascend, ascend, and I will greet thee at the pearly gates"?

"No more grass, no more speed, no more shit. I got Jesus," screamed a fellow from the left side of the tent. Soon a chorus of voices followed his lead. Footstamping and fingersnapping accompanied the declarations for Jesus. The rock group sang some more. Another girl saw Jesus. A boy ran to the platform and fainted, so we never found out what he'd seen. I was tired. It was very hot, but to leave seemed impossible.

At last the preacher said, "To end this meeting I will give a special blessing to all those who have seen Jesus tonight. Let them come forward and take hands."

A group rushed up, a line formed, waiting to reach the platform. I stood up, ready to push my way out of the tent.

I leaned down to tell Sarah we would leave. She pulled her hand out of mine and ran like a child chasing a hat in the wind across the seated people to the line in front of the platform. I watched her wait her turn, a pale little girl with a fierce look in her face. I knew she was telling the preacher she believed in Jesus. He smiled and hugged her, and she left the platform, came back to me, and quietly, without a word, we went into the dark field illuminated only by a random star and the lights of cigarettes, as others crossed and re-crossed the ground, looking for their cars. We found ours. I started the motor, and we drove into Cambridge to the Daisy Motel that had been expecting us some hours earlier. Sarah fell asleep in the back of the car.

AFTER I HAD TAKEN our suitcases into the room, I opened the back of the car and tried to lift her in my arms. I couldn't pick her up. The time for cradling was over. I woke her. She was half asleep. She found the bed, kicked off her sneakers and lay down.

"Are you mad, Mother, that I saw Jesus?"

"No," I said, "what was He like in person?"

Bad blood, my grandmother would have said, sitting in her velvet chair looking out at the brick walls of Marion Avenue in the Bronx. Bad blood poisons the whole system. What could I do? Transfusing Sarah totally would not fix what was wrong.

I went into the lobby of the motel and bought a pack

of cigarettes. The lobby smelled of ammonia and Ajax and cheap perfume. I hurried back to the room, which also smelled of a pine-scented toilet-bowl cleanser. I changed into my nightgown. At night I always felt the cold edges of my body as it thrashed about on the single bed. I could scream with the need to be touched with hands other than my own.

"Mother," said Sarah, "I don't really believe in Jesus. I didn't see Him or anything. I just wanted to say so like everybody else."

"I understand," I said. "It's a wish, not a lie. Don't worry about it." I felt exhilarated. Sarah had spoken to me, told me a secret of her soul, and perhaps a bridge between us, a little love, remained. Then again maybe she had really seen Jesus and just didn't want to offend me, knowing my rational agnostic prejudice—maybe she's just biding her time, and one day she'll run off to Lourdes and throw away the millstone of her mother and be truly saved. Is she a Marrano, or a turncoat? Either way, she's a conformist, interchangeable with all the other little girls at Miss Lennitt's School. "Sarah," I said, "you can believe anything you like, your mind is free and its thoughts are yours to ride wherever they take you."

"Don't worry, Mother, I really don't believe in anything at all." She turned over, and soon I could tell from the child's even breathing she was asleep.

I had gone to the same Sunday school where my mother had received her Jewish education—some of the teachers remembered her. I didn't want to hear about her—it frightened me to feel that history was repeating itself, as if I had no time or space of my own, but was merely planned as a repetition or a second chance, like a string of paper dolls, a string of females identical, attached across the tragic Jewish history we learned in Mr. Birnbaum's class. Each Sunday we would discuss another pogrom, a diaspora, an exile, a genocide attempt, and on the bulletin board in the tiny room where we all sat cramped together in the basement hung *Life* magazine photographs of the liberation of Auschwitz and Dachau. We huddled together, crushed by the weight of human sorrow: of homes destroyed, dishes broken, treasures left behind; of murdered sons and disease-ridden fathers; of starving babies and raped women bleeding to death in burning barns. The images piled up like the stones of the pharaoh's pyramid, and Mr. Birnbaum would always say as he closed the class, "It makes you proud to be Jewish, doesn't it?"

My second year of Sundays with Mr. Birnbaum I began to wonder, proud of what? A capacity to survive, to suffer? An endless pain, an insecurity bred into the bones, bones that expect to be crunched in the next social upheaval? Why be proud of being the victim? The roasted goat doesn't taste good to himself. I sat there listening to tales of the wisdom of Rabbi Hillel, of the courage of the Maccabees, of the martyrdom of the Jewish merchants who were captured by the Spanish Inquisition, of iron maidens closing on Torah scholars, of rabbis without fingernails going mad in rat-infested dungeons, and I planned an escape—a painless genocide, a pleasure-filled life that would guarantee the future would hold no terrors of persecution. Marry out—each little Jewish girl had an obligation to marry out, and then, and only then the children might be safe and the terrible tale of Jewish history would be done. No large values, tradition, scholarship, holiness, would cover for me the basic craziness, stubbornness of a survival that imposed an unchosen suffering on the great-grandchildren to come. My grandfather was interested in my politics of womb eradication, but my grandmother was so shocked she put her hands over her ears whenever I approached the subject with her. Mr. Birnbaum wanted to throw me out of class, and eventually by some mutual decision my Jewish education was discontinued.

Rachel, Rachel, the wait is too long. Weep, Leah, weep for being first and ugly; both weep for being cattle traded two for one on the open market. Powerless to choose, to run away into the long desert, no god outside your father's house, helpless before your husband's pleasure or displeasure; breasts will sag, and infections gray your vaginal lips, but you must live according to the schedules of law and ritual and give the obedience demanded of any domestic animal. Weep far away from the Torah, weep away from the holy center of the men's world, because the Lord God, Jehovah, the nameless name of all names, does not like menstruating women whose blood is after all only their own. Weep for being unclean, weep for being born Jewish when Philistines copulated freely beneath the stars and bled without shame about the family fires. Weep because your sons will feel sanctified only in places their mother is forbidden. Weep for centuries of pain, none of your choosing; always you are cleaning pots, lighting candles or putting away linen when the pogrom starts—the Cossacks, the Turks, the Romans, the Germans, the Gentiles, come and pulverize you and yours, while your men with long shawls kiss the hem of God's thought. In the end you believe in nothing at all, like Sarah, and perhaps like Sarah your eyes are dry.

THE NEXT DAY we headed out on Route 60. I avoided the main section of town, and very quickly we were riding on a flat road bordered by small brush forests; an occasional clearing revealed farms and black-and-white cows grazing in the sunlight. I saw a young girl with blonde braids walking along, swinging a stick. Was she going into the woods to meet her boyfriend home on leave from the Marines? Would she conceive and die some months from now on the abortionist's table in nearby Columbus, or was she merely picking wild berries for the breakfast table?

Manuelo Desprito was the name of the Mexican lawyer I was to call when I had crossed the border. He would take me to Juarez's City Hall, sign papers and bring me before the judge who would grant the decree, severing by foreign law what had already been broken. Why go through with the charade—the form of social commerce? I could turn the car around. We could still go to the Cape for the summer. We could walk on the dunes, watching the waves and the gulls. We could have cookouts and picnic lunches with friends who would considerately invite us, knowing we lived without a man in a solitude that was worse in the evening but heavy in the crisp early morning. "Poor Emily," they would say, "she suffered so long. I imagine she knew about his girls—but artists, you know, are not meant for conventional molds." The summer could be used up without any special event, just time passed like paper towels sponging and mopping till the months were gone. I could turn the car back to the safe shape of summers we had known—sand in the hair and the sheets, a single white steeple appearing over the hill, the prick of Christian virtue, the geometrically correct New England house, in which squares and wide beams balance in cool harmony, the gray shingles covering, disguising, the more Romanesque or Gothic thoughts of the inhabitants. But the car keeps moving forward, not just because I have an appointment with Manuelo Desprito, but I have promised myself that my world will open and the forms of things change, and there will be no returning, no hovering about the empty nest, or haunting the places where he had walked. Just a new single existence like a kite broken from its string moving upwards in the drafts till its spot of color disappears. Manuelo, I am on my way. I want to legally return to myself and hold papers in my hand that tell me I am betraying no one if I sleep on the floor of a bar with a thousand-and-one sailors.

I am bragging, of course. I am still shy and won't act in a way my grandmother would not understand, if not approve. Esther, whore to Ahasueras, enemy of Haman, brave adopted daughter of Mordecai, what a marvelous time you must have had, sporting on the royal sheets, showing off your round bottom and saving the Jewish people temporarily from yet another disaster. You did win them time in bed. Sex is a military art, therefore your progeny learned to use it and not just to give in full appetite or naive joy. Hurray for Queen Esther! When I was a child, on each Purim holiday we had a costume party, and all the little girls dressed in Persian pants and harem scarves, eager to sacrifice our virginity to save the property and well-being of the Jewish community. I could not wait to be chosen for my beauty to spread my legs for Ahasueras, the uncircumcised flap of his penis tied down like a huge winding sheet covering the dead. It would wave and dance above my head while I seduced my king and master—whore and heroine for once and only once combined.

Sarah played jacks in the back of the car, her ball bouncing in what seemed like perfect rhythm—Pigs in the Pen, Chickens in the Coop, Follow My Fancy Number Four—"I did it," she would call out in triumph every now and then. I followed the road; no hitchhikers today. The hot sun made the asphalt damp and soft in places, and the white lines seemed uncertain in the hot dusty haze that hung above them. We were headed toward Springfield. Mile by mile we were moving away from the coast into the middle land where the true Americans, the real builders of the dream, came, planned, schemed, and incorporated, shouted good-sounding phrases into the long sky that stretched low over the land.

The June corn was beginning to sprout in wide fields on both sides of the empty highway. Green shoots calf-high waved in the warm wind. A crow, several sparrows, flew near, following their own inexplicable routes. Up ahead suddenly, a billboard, "Hot Dogs at Horace's—Two Thousand Yards Ahead." A red-faced freckled child is trying to take away a hot dog, mustard flying, from an eager black-and-white spotted puppy, whose red elongated tongue flickers across the board. And then another billboard, "Fifty Miles: Springfield's Finest Motel Historic Site." Houses started to appear, pinks, blues, ranch, Tech-built with plastic swimming tubs in the yards. Swings and jungle gyms sprouted like dandelions as the houses got closer and closer together. We were in the suburbs of Springfield. The road narrowed. Traffic lights decorated low poles every few blocks. There were pizza parlors, used-car lots, gas stations, a large discount carpet store, a housing project eight stories high, carefully geometrically planned—already the windows were broken and the green paint on the doors chipped. "Frankie Fucks" was written in great white painted letters on the side of one building. We drove slowly past a kiddie amusement center with pinball machines and a cotton candy dispenser, empty lots with broken bottles, and a little store that claimed to be "Madame Ravina's—Wedding Gowns at Great Savings." The faces on the sidewalk were black. We drove on over a little bridge that crossed a small muddy river into downtown Springfield. The faces were white again. The street was neat, with geraniums potted in the windows and a restaurant called "Ma Petite" where I decided we would stop for lunch.

My grandmother would have disapproved of divorce. "A woman's bed is to lie in, what else?" she had said. She had believed that America was the perfected revolution, that the gradual acquisition of possessions undreamed of in a Russian girlhood meant that the inequities of the world, the injustices her husband inveighed against, were coming to an end, and her very own china closet proved that progress was here. If not the Messiah, if not dancing in the street, at least a practical kind of goodness shone down from the heavens and gave her lace doilies and tortoise-shell fans and velvet curtains and good quality sheets to make the bed she didn't seem unwilling to lie on.

I always think of her sitting on a large upholstered chair, looking out the window. The streets of the Upper Bronx were always crowded and noisy with shoppers, peddlers and school children coming and going, women carrying packages, pushing carriages, and gathering to talk. And underneath the elevated train, in the shadows where the sunlight fell in squares on the cobblestones below, Michael and I and my friend Xenia played like animals in cages, howling and screeching at one another, lions and tigers and monkeys. Grandma kept the five small rooms of our apartment so shiny that it was a place no devil, imp or gnome would feel comfortable in visiting. To get there, I walked up five hundred and ten narrow cement steps. The apartment buildings were tiered along the sharp embankments of the Bronx. As in the back alleys of little towns in Italy, it was necessary to climb a small mountain to reach the gray entrance of our building, identical in form and shape to the thousand other buildings that made together a charmed circle, a Jewish neighborhood, a world of old women whose ankles swelled in the day, whose teeth came out at night, and whose ungrateful daughters never did anything right.

My mother and father had been eradicated on the West Side Highway. Off for a week's vacation in Atlantic City, they had been hit by a truck delivering mattresses, whose driver, drunk or crazy, had jumped the lane divider headed for a suicide in the Hudson River. I was staying at my grandmother's, a baby so young I cannot remember, and they never returned. My grandparents often reassured me that they didn't regret the opportunity to begin again with me.

I had my mother's old room—her childhood books waited on the shelf for me to grow old enough to read. Sometimes at night I felt as if the hills of the Bronx were hollow caves, and ghosts of dead relations burrowed like moles beneath the apartment buildings, never able to find a way out to the sun, to the living, a network of prisoners hacking away with hands, nails, teeth, at the dirt and the stone of the ground beneath. In the basement where I would take the wash down to the machines, I would listen for the sounds of the dead always too far away to reach me.

"Ma Petite" turned out not to be a very French restaurant, after all. Broiled chicken and roast beef was all there was. I ordered wine. It came in a water glass and tasted like toothpaste. Sarah had a sandwich and bought a post card from the restaurant to send to her father. I tried not to think about him as she wrote—to forget the way he played in the bathtub, pushing the soap around as if it were a toy boat, the way he would stand at the window—"Zap, Zap, Zap," he would point with a finger turned into a ray gun. "You out there are all paralyzed and at my mercy. Zap, Zap, Zap, I killed them all," he would shout triumphantly. The paintings turned to squares of blues and greens as if the sea had been distilled of erratic life and only its formal proportions remained, reflected as God might have seen it before He permitted the first aquatic cell to feed on its cold and wet surround. He was painting five or six hours a day, and silent, whiskey-filled, another three. I fed him and touched him gently. I thought I was his inspiration, a force of art like Aphrodite floating in the Grecian air. Actually I was a nurse whose thankless profession was chosen out of guilt and morbid curiosity, a hanger-on of human suffering.

By infinitely admiring the work put before me, by hiding rejections, avoiding unfriendly critics, by providing supper and sex and art supplies and contacts in the art world, I offered the blood that fueled the work; like Dracula's victim, I lay prone and still, my veins exposed, enjoying every moment of the peculiar gluing together of fang and neck.

The blood, they say, of Jewish maidens turns Dracula into an intellectual, a perceiver of the abstract laws of evil. No silver cross protects the Jewess, only the sometime strength of her will to survive allows her to defang the monster so that its bare pink gums are rendered harmless as an infant's. But I had loved Alex and clung like a baby monkey. I sat outside his studio waiting for him to finish and look at me, a toad with peculiar tumorous brown bumps and webbed feet, a lizard under the rock whose slimy skin protected a hot heart that beat so fast it soon expired, an earthworm cut in two, each part desperate for regeneration—and so I loved him. Like the toilet that doesn't flush well enough, a repeat of his image floats in my brain.

Of course, after the baby was born it was different. I was a changed person—never entirely a single self, always now paired with the baby. Then when Alex left me home to go out with his friends, I felt a purpose to it all. I was at least anchored to another being who smiled at my approach, whose hands reached up, pulling at my earrings, rubbing the soft wool of my sweater. One night when Sarah was three, before she started nursery school, I asked Alex if he was glad we had a child. A strange sad look came over his face.

"As she grows," he said, "I get nearer death—it's a reminder that I have to paint fast because my time is short."

I loved him for his pain, for his vulnerability, for his paintings. "But what about Sarah? Are you glad to have Sarah?"

"Who chooses?" he said; "I would have been happy alone, but," he shrugged wearily, "who chooses? You're really a bourgeoise," he said, "always thinking in illustrations, a car stuffed with groceries, a spaniel dog's ears blowing in the wind, freckle-faced kids flying kites while Mommy and Daddy fix peanut butter sandwiches by a bubbling brook."

He was right! My secret images were of an America I had never known, and my inevitable disappointments were biting me like July mosquitoes after a heavy rain.

AFTER LUNCH Sarah and I checked into the Lewis and Clark, the best hotel in town. Each floor had a different color scheme, and we were allowed to pick a red, white or blue suite. The theme of the hotel was Early American; George Washington crossing the Delaware appeared on the curtains, the bedspreads, and the dresser doily. We chose a blue floor, and even the bath towels and the bars of soap were blue. After the modern motel, it seemed almost as if we had returned to the Plaza in New York. The bar was called the Jefferson Room, the dining room was called the Madison Maisonette, and the cashier's office had a sign above it lettered "Hamilton's Haven." I forced Sarah to change into a dress and braided her hair in honor of our more formal surroundings.

Once out on the front porch of the hotel, the heat of the city fell on us like a hostile hand. The afternoon stretched out, contentless. I thought I had done enough driving and we would stay in Springfield for a day, a place where once years ago pioneers from the eastern coast had gathered to buy their covered wagons, to stock up necessary supplies, to change their horses for newer or stronger ones, and finally to load their trunks, settle their rifles, ride down the main street of Springfield out into the open prairie of the West, where a man could go five hundred miles across the waving grass without finding another man or a single building. . . .

"Let's go upstairs," said Sarah. "Let's turn on the air conditioner and watch television. Maybe 'Dark Shadows' is playing out here, or 'To Tell the Truth' or 'Dating Game.' I want to go in," she whined, but I was not crossing the country to sit in front of an electronic tube and, lying on cool, clean bedsheets, let time, like cement blocks tied to a stool pigeon's leg, drag me down to an early death.

I called for the car, and the doorman, dressed in buckskin and coon cap, drops of sweat on his pimpled nose, brought it around. I had looked through the Traveler's Information at the hotel desk and realized Springfield had no museum, no old homes open to the public, no zoo, no gardens, no special industry (a shoe factory had closed several years before, leaving broken windows and empty stone floors behind). "Sarah," I said, "we are going to the one and only tourist spot in Springfield out of town to see the statue, a gift of the Daughters of the American Revolution, the Ohio chapter." Mrs. Mamie Dustin, chairman of the local division, personally brought fresh flowers to the foot of the statue every second Tuesday of each month of the year in memory of her mother, who had also been president of the organization in her time.

It wasn't much of an outing. It wasn't a distraction Sarah would accept as worthy of the heat or the loss of good television time, but I had a kind of nagging curiosity. Mrs. Mamie Dustin must live in one of those big white houses on the fancy side of town where the streets had names like Buckle, Pump, Oxford, Saddle, Boot, in honor of the shoe factory's products that must have been once affectionately regarded by the townsfolk. Somewhere out over the ridge of the paved streets, I knew there was a country club, a golf course, tennis lessons for kids, a swimming pool, and a pro who flexed his muscles in the afternoon for small groups of women who played the eighteen holes hoping each day the circle they walked would bring them to another beginning, a lower handicap, better cards, another bed.

Sarah said, "I want to go swimming. What kind of summer is it without water? Why can't we go to a hotel that has a pool? Why didn't you ever think of that?"

"We will, Sarah," I promised. "Next time I won't stop anywhere that doesn't have a pool. I promise."

She was quiet. I felt guilty. It would be a fine day for a child to rush the waves at Quannacut Beach on the Cape. The water would still be June cold, and the children would cry with pleasure and terror as they were splashed by the foam as it sprayed over the sand. It would be a fine day for a child to lean against her father's shoulder and scan the horizon for fishing boats, white sails or gray smokestacks, coming through the waves like small ungranted wishes, wishes made on a multitude of stars and birthday cakes.

We turned on Route 40 out of town. Soon there were

farms on the roadside, chickens running around on the bare dirt, and pick-up trucks packed with large rusty tools. There was an automobile graveyard at the edge of the road, a metal mountain of dead cars. I thought I heard a groaning of the mangled steel and chrome and realized it was a train whistle on the tracks a mile or so to the left. The land was flat, like unleavened bread, like the Passover matzohs hidden by my grandfather every year; always, because he was old and forgetful, he hid it in the same place so I could easily find it, behind the clock my grandmother had bought for my mother's wedding present and had then reclaimed for her own mantel.

We passed a large brick building set back from the road, "The 4-H Club—Worldwide Headquarters." Trucks, cars, children, overflowed a small parking lot. I thought of stopping, of taking a tour, but felt out of place in such a wholesome grouping. Grass-roots Americans might not welcome a divorcée from New York of immigrant stock whose knowledge of farms came from elementary school readers that showed pink-cheeked farmers leaning on pitchforks plunged deep into piles of golden hay. I drove on. We passed a sign pointing to the Indian village of Piqua, where, the sign told us, the Battle of Piqua had been fought in 1780. The British and their Shawnee allies had been defeated. Now there would be no village, no Shawnees, no Redcoats, only ghosts in the space of what had been destroyed. My head ached, and I felt tracer bullets ranging across the highway, cruising not for me or Sarah but for participants in battles that could never be forgotten.

We came to the Madonna of the Trail monument. It was off the main highway, inside a clump of maple and oak trees. We parked the car and walked on the damp earth about a quarter of a mile into the woods, and there was the Madonna. Not Mary in robes of ancient times, but a pioneer lady with a straight nose, a poke bonnet, a basket of food over one arm, and a gown that the sculptor had clearly indicated was patched calico. The lady stood on a high pedestal, at the base of which lay a dozen wilting roses, a gift, I knew, of Mrs. Mamie Dustin.

Sarah looked for a moment. "All right, Mother, now let's go back to the hotel."

"In a little while," I said.

I knew the quality of the artwork would not have startled Madison Avenue, appeared in the Whitney, the Guggenheim or the Modern, but I could see it standing in the Metropolitan a thousand years from now, excavated by some anthropologist, specialist in the Twentieth Century. It could stand respectably next to the head of Nefertiti or a sarcophagus or a medieval sculpture of the real Madonna, and the crassness of line, the stiffness of limb, the dullness in the facial expression, could be explained and admired as an example of the primitive art of a primitive people—an earth goddess, clearly, a harvest figure (see the basket of fruit), a votive statue signifying birth (notice the fullness of dress around the stomach).

A stone lady standing in the middle of nowhere on the site of trails that had grown over with split-level developments—a pioneer woman: I looked into her honest face. I felt a love, a surge of worship, such as must overwhelm Mrs. Dustin each time she bends down to place her flowers. After all, I was staring at the stone embalmment of a basic American truth. The West was won by such ladies, leaving their mothers, their sewing circles in Boston or Charleston or Wilmington, and following their propertyless menfolk out into the land, enduring the Indians, enduring the cold deserted winters, into a future of hardship and work. Women bearing babies in the backs of rolling wagons, coyotes howling in the distance, campfire lights flickering, Indians shrieking and yelling, hatchets flying, bears and foxes stalking the young ones. The West was taken by women on their backs in beds carried from eastern cities into the wilderness, giving birth to survivors of typhoid and smallpox, mumps, measles, meningitis, falling blades, hurricanes, lightning, wild animals, gunshot wounds, Indians, bad crops, no rain, great floods, locusts, ants, dust storms, outlaws, bandits, thieves. No wonder the lines under the eyes of the statue are so deep, and numbness, the result of too much fear, freezes the mouth into a hard bitter line. But the women who went West, great-great grandmothers of the present Daughters of the American Revolution—they had something quite extraordinary, those ladies. They had a duality. Life was hard and small and mean and wearing. It was short and brutal, and the work was backbreaking, the rewards fleeting; as in peasant life the world over, each effort was done, undone, and redone—but at the same time, all this petty human activity was making a new country, was spreading the civilization, such as it was, into the four corners of the continent. Big work for ladies, the most important part of it done on the mattresses where the breeding took place.

To have a historic purpose, to breathe and pant and heave a child into the future, to build a new society—I felt jealous of the stone statue whose life had had purpose, enemy and friend—not like mine, that of a wandering Jewess, covering the globe, belonging only peripherally to one culture or another, a grandmother who collected china, knowing alien boots could and would smash it all to bits a week, a century later. Perhaps contemporary Jewish women should form their own society, Daughter of Refugees of the Ongoing-Universal-Endless Upheaval. We could meet on boats, three miles out to sea, and not allow anyone whose ancestors had lived in less than four countries to join.

"Come on, Mother, it's hot and buggy here. Let's go back to the hotel; I'm hungry. I'm being bitten; let's go."

Sarah was right about the bugs. I decided I wanted to leave the monument a present in the best of the Judeo-Christian tradition. I opened my pocketbook, rummaging around to see what I could give her, and found my Bonwit Teller charge card, my Master Charge card, among the paraphernalia that surfaced. What better present for a pioneer lady than a card of entry to the ease and comfort of the modern world? Electric eggbeaters, wall ovens, garbage-disposals, could all be hers. I climbed over the little rail and reached up to place my cards at her feet.

"Just a minute. What are you doing, lady?" a righteous, angry male voice shouted. I was startled and took an instinctive step forward away from the voice, and immediately fell over a corner of the pedestal. I went down on the ground, writhing with both pain and embarrassment. My skirt was up too high, I could tell my shins were bruised and bleeding, and my chin and jaw were hurt, swelling to huge heights even as I raised myself to a sitting position.

"Oh, Mother," said Sarah, walking away, "there was no reason to trip over such a big monument."

I felt hot sweaty hands lifting me up and saw a uniformed state guard in cowboy hat with pistol slung low over his hips.

"Look, lady, I'm here to see that no one defaces this statue. You can take pictures. You can eat sandwiches and throw your trash in that big can over there, but the law of Ohio does not allow defacing of monuments, expectorating on monuments, or any mutilation of public property."

I saw my bleeding shins were dirt-stained; my dripping chin I mopped with my sleeve. And I tried to assure the policeman that never in my life had I written "Emily Was Here" or "Emily and Alex 1952" or "Emily Sucks" above my telephone number or anything at all on public property.

I am not a defacer of countrysides, a spoiler of landscapes, a secret graffiti writer. I'm a humble person without pretense of immortality or fame. All I want is to get to Mexico.

"What a thing to teach a child, to mark up public property. Some people have no respect." The guard obviously did not believe me.

"Right now in Springfield," I told the policeman, "some little old lady is being hit on the head with a lead pipe because you're out here protecting this Madonna. If you don't leave me alone, I'll charge police brutality. I'll call all the national papers, and they'll just have to look at me, and they'll know what kind of police you have in Ohio."

"All right, lady, calm down." He backed off, adjusting his gun on his hip the way a lady straightens her stockings after an unfortunate sexual encounter.

Sarah had waited for me down the road. "You look terrible," she said. "You look like you've been fighting." A cold dislike entered her voice. "What were you doing, Mother? Writing on the pedestal?" she asked.

"I don't have to tell you everything," I said, feeling guilty of a host of crimes, feeling small and without authority. I thought it was exactly time to go back to the hotel and turn on the television set.

Driving to town, I thought of my friend Susannah, who cried whenever she spoke of her daughter Marion. Last summer at Cape Ann her seventeen-year-old daughter got a waitress job with a school friend at a nearby hotel. It was a sailing-fishing resort town with a lot of kids who gathered on the main street near the drugstore—Susannah had thought it would be a good space of shared time, the last before her daughter went off to college. She invited her daughter's friend to join them for the summer so that companionship would not be a problem. The girls started the summer enthusiastically, admiring the tall masts of the boats that slowly moved about the harbor like dimly remembered secrets between best friends. But then it appeared the girls didn't like the boys in town, or perhaps the boys had other girls. Someone started a cruel rumor that the two girls were narcotics agents, and many of the young people turned away as they approached. Marion began to eat a lot, french fries and pizza, and her backside broadened till it was wide and full like the bottom of a rowboat. Her face broke out in splotches. She wore a torn pair of jeans and a workshirt to hide her body and refused to go to the beach any more, because it was "boring," because there were no boys, and because she was tight and angry and no longer able to jump the waves, screaming with pleasure as she rode over the white foam. Now she moved like a tugboat in shallow circles blowing black smoke into the air.

Susannah said whenever she came into the house and the girls were there, she tensed like a mouse that feels the hawk about—the girls stopped their conversation in the middle when the mother appeared and went into their room, slamming the door. They sat down to dinner with sullen looks, with angry bangings, and said nothing through family meals that grew so long and arduous that when at last the girls had gone back to their room and wild giggles could be heard in the kitchen, Susannah would sit on a chair hugging herself to keep from crying. So deep was the pain in her, it was as if a large fishhook meant for tuna or big blues had plunged into her insides, pulling her softly along lonely waters.

One day there was a final argument—a misunderstanding, actually. Susannah came back from the beach, from a lovely long afternoon of finding shells to make necklaces for the younger girls, an afternoon of blueberry picking on low bushes, and with the illustrations planned for a children's book she had started.

Marion was waiting for her. "I can't communicate with you, I hate you, fuck you, fuck you." In the language of today's anger, the girl turned on her mother, a lifetime of accusation in her eyes, and a hatred that now like the division between earth and sky lay between them, a sharp uncrossable line.

"A human being has a choice," Susannah told me. "She doesn't have to like me—she's not an infant who needs me—she has chosen to shut herself away, to never let me know the last names of her friends, or to tell me any thought or dreams that might be a part of her. We talk across the barricades, stiffly, suspiciously, as if translating each sentence from Arabic. There are reasons for all this—a seventeen-year web of relationship. I wake at night and go over it all: what I said, what she said, what I did to her—that I left her father, that I stayed with him too long—I think it all over, over and over again, but I never understand it quite. She is free to hate me, and now I feel in return a fury rise within me, a desire to slam a door in her face, to cast a secret look at my friend; to ruin her summer, her winter, her spring; to make her feel as she and her friend have made me feel, an unwelcome stranger in my house."

"Adolescence," I said to my friend Susannah, "will go away."

"No," she said, "you don't understand. She hates me and we will never be friends. The wound is too grave and never heals, it ulcerates on and on. I look at the younger girls," Susannah said, "and try to prepare myself for an old age of watching television, of sitting on a bed I cannot leave, littered with orange peels, talking to myself as though I were another voice—one really needs another voice."

My friend Susannah was inconsolable, and I thought of her all the way back to Springfield.

Later that day we dressed up and went to the Madison Maisonette for dinner. I looked at my daughter across the white tablecloth and all the glittering crystal reflecting the green candles that flickered in hurricane lamps of some period or other. My grandmother used to take me to Schrafft's on Fordham Road on special occasions. I would order giant sodas and little sandwiches with the crusts removed. I always felt bored and fascinated at the same time: bored by how long it took to get the food, and fascinated by my grandmother's conversation, which was usually a retelling of neighborhood catastrophes. Mr. Greenburg had had a stroke in the middle of the night, and the ambulance had stalled on the Third Avenue Bridge. And Mrs. Hoffman's eyesight could only last another three weeks, which was no wonder, the terrible things she'd seen! And always my grandmother would talk about other people's daughters, about the pain they gave their parents by moving to San Francisco or Paris, the puny grandchildren they produced, the weasels of sons-in-law they brought home. My mother's death was mourned in such indirect ways day after day, and I was not quite enough to undo or redo the past.

Sarah was bored with me. Her eyes wandered over the room, looking for something of interest. The other diners —traveling salesmen, an elderly woman with her nurse companion, a few middle-aged couples celebrating a birthday, several dentists attending a convention—did not seem to amuse her. She kicked at her chair leg in a kind of desperation, in a frustrated desire to curl up on the bed watching The Partridge Family, My Three Sons, The Flip Wilson Show. She was humming commercials to herself. I searched for conversation, my mind as frantically empty as on my first dates with scrawny, eager boys. At last the dessert, a marvelous ice cream parfait, arrived, and Sarah brightened as we discussed the relative virtues of sundaes, banana splits and chocolate cake.

After dinner Sarah went up to the room, and I went into the Jefferson Room. A divorcée has to learn to walk in the adult world; without a mate at her elbow, she is exposed on all sides to attack and rejection. But I knew I could not wait for Alex any more but would have to go alone.

Now I was a participant in a peculiar game in which I would be both the hunter and the hunted. I had put make-up on my chin and slacks over my shins, but still I felt bruised, an apple fallen too far, too hard, too soon from its beloved tree.

I sat down in a little black booth where the lighting was protectively bad. The music was piped in overhead, old Beatles songs of another era. A face appeared in front of mine; a nametag on his lapel told me he was with the dentists.

"H. Moore," he said. "May I join you?"

I smiled. What else was I doing in the bar? He introduced himself. Cambridge was his home. He was the only oral periodonist for miles around, and he liked to keep up with his colleagues. I told him where I was going and why. He leered. I could see him figuring an easy score, one to tell the boys in the locker room. I told him I was Jewish—a little tension might make the encounter more interesting. "Oh, you sexy thing," he said, chucking me hard on my scraped chin. He showed me pictures of his wife and children, who looked clean, pressed, and eager for a trip to the supermarket. He liked dogs a lot, and we traded animal stories. I told him about my last sick cat and how it had died of gallstones because the vet was ignorant and uncaring. He sympathized, and he had a nice face, a smile that spoke of campfires and fishing trips. And he looked like the kind of guy who carried the Christmas tree home from the store for his kids and stayed up all night setting up the electric train. But was I really ready to roll in the hay, to hit the sack, to pound the butter, whatever, with a strange penis I did not love or like or know?

I thought till I was nineteen that all sexual feelings were

to be banished till at last, like a good dam, they would irrigate the marriage bed. But now at thirty-five I would not, could not, be prisoner of the ghetto of my childhood; the moralities that no one paid any attention to any more were, like the stories of dybbuks and the imps, simply tales to scare impressionable children out of their legitimate share in the pleasure of the body. My grandmother didn't talk to me for two weeks after she found Lotte and me dancing naked in my mother's room.

H. Moore, I thought to myself, you and I will make a little liberation, why not? A few drinks later, a medley of songs from The Rolling Stones later, suggestions from the rock culture had reached my pelvis. H. Moore, I'm ready. Moore went back to his table to boast to his colleagues he had snared a Jewish bird. I went back to the room to find Sarah watching the Late Show; seven survivors of a sinking ship were sitting around in a life raft, discussing whom they should eat. I went to the bathroom, and though it slipped and squirmed away, I recaptured the diaphragm, inserted it, and stepped forward to meet H. Moore on his own ground. I've protected myself, I thought proudly—never rely on a man. The issue of such a beastly moment would surely have scales and horns and eyes that rolled backwards in its head.

As I waited for the elevator, I thought of Judith off to visit the tent of Holofernes. The lovely Judith draws her knife and kills the enemy general whose eager erection collapses as blood drains from his wound. Clever Jewish woman, has she murdered a true enemy of her people, or has she merely deprived herself of a long night of pleasure? What happened to her after? No respectable young man would marry her, since she was not necessarily a virgin and had been at least exposed to another male. Besides, a girl who pulls a knife is not the kind most fellows want. So Judith was tainted property; she probably mourned her life away, a maiden aunt, a visitor in other people's homes, a war hero without a medal.

I went to H. Moore's red room. The bedspread was red, the floor, the ceiling, the familiar print of George Washington crossing the Delaware—it was like being inside the womb on a menstrual day, the placenta crumbling, sweeping away deteriorating cellular matter. H. Moore opened a bottle of Scotch, fixed himself a drink and took off his shoes.

"Some day, baby," he said, "we're going to live in a cavityless world—a little fluoride, a chemical shell on the teeth, and a perfect set of white choppers will be everybody's birthright. That's why I invest in real estate. The day is coming when oral surgery will be shelved like leech treatment or mustard plaster—I'm salting it away in a reclaimable swamp, you're not looking at a stupid dentist."

I could tell that he needed admiration and reassurance. He wasn't a male stud, a horse out into the field to back into any female if the time is right and the smell is in the air.

He probably wished he were just a penis, cut off from a brain that flooded with images of his wife buying charcoal briquets, of his children splashing in the country-club pool. He didn't want to be inhibited by worries about whether or not I had syphilis or any other communicable New York disease.

I undressed, I smoked a cigarette, he undressed and turned the light low—what is illicit is more fun if it is barely seen. He touched my face—I winced; he had again chopped my sore chin in an affectionate gesture. He started to sweat, though I felt the air conditioner was making the room cold, and I had to resist a desire to get under the covers. I told him how clever I thought he was to invest in real estate, how smart he had been to specialize in oral surgery and periodontal work. I admired the wiry hair on his chest, and the fine strong muscles in his legs, which he told me came from using the Exercycle his wife had given him on his last birthday.

At last he began to stroke me and I felt surges of excitement, mechanical, as if a clever Masters and Johnson were at me; but nevertheless physiology is not always delicate, and I felt my body, no longer cold, but beautiful, mobile, the essence of woman alive in all the right organs, stirring deep in the center, a joy—I could be animal, not Emily Brimberg Johnson, just a girl, just Jane swinging on the vines of an African forest—all the pleasures of promiscuity could be mine. There, Grandma, the hell with my reputation, the hell with saving it for marriage—I have come of age and may never love anyone again, so let them whisper about me in dental circles all over Ohio, I don't care! I twisted, turned and moved a long while, I touched and played. After a while, I realized H. Moore's penis had remained a small limp tongue with nothing to say. It hung over his wrinkled balls, clinging flat to his body like a lollipop stick to a child's clothes.

I stopped feeling like Jane and started to work—I didn't want the failure to be mine, I tried and tried, but after another thirty-five minutes I dropped back on the red bed in exhaustion. It wasn't going to be. I reached for my cigarettes. H. Moore rolled over to his side of the bed and closed his eyes. I got up, got dressed and was about to tiptoe out of the room, leaving him undisturbed, when he turned over, sat up and gave me an accusing look. "It's because you have bad breath," he said. "Bad breath is the one thing that turns me off. I'm very sensitive to it." With that he lay down again and closed his eyes.

I went back to our blue room and found Sarah watching the Late, Late Show, Marlon Brando parading around like a southern sheriff. "I don't care what you've been doing," Sarah said, without moving her eyes from an airlines commercial.

"I don't care what you've been doing, either," I said with irritation.

Immediately I felt an anxiety, a guilt, a grief that flooded my entire spirit. I hadn't meant to be sharp. I had in fact left my little girl for hours in a strange hotel room in the middle of the country with no friend to call and talk with, no mother to turn the covers down and switch off the light. She had probably been frightened of the immense unknown, of the wide world that she could not yet negotiate. She was collecting traumas to reveal to her analyst one day.

"Darling," I said, "good night." I bent over to kiss her. She moved away. Bad breath? I went into the bathroom, brushed my teeth and, exhausted, went to bed, falling instantly asleep.

EARLY IN THE MORNING, after a quick breakfast of soggy bacon and greasy eggs, we started out again. Sarah had found that the hotel's manager's office sold comics, and I allowed her to buy several. Her choices all involved a character named Archie, his girlfriend Veronica and a bald-headed school principal. It seemed innocent enough, but I couldn't help feeling as I glanced at her through the rear-view mirror that I could drop her off at any stop along the route and she could adapt, culturally merge with her fellow Americans, more easily than I. She was the strange conformist product of a union that had temporarily merged several traditions. The result of mixing blue and red appeared to be a bland white. I decided to keep driving past Indianapolis, which I knew would just be a city with nothing but brick universities to distinguish it from the other towns along the way, and head for Terre Haute, which had a mysterious and beautiful name—it made me think of dark Mexican girls swinging gold-braceleted arms, beckoning cowboys into mirrored bars with whiskey bottles lined on shelves, and dancing music played on an old broken-down spinet.

Terre Haute, high land, where Indians had come to exchange skins for guns and settlers had passed on, not finding it far enough away. The land was fertile all right, but the ones with restless spirit who saw themselves at the pinnacle rode on to the mangrove forests of California, while the ones with middling ambition stopped and prospered or failed in Terre Haute.

I drove fast now at 70 mph, my eyes riveted to the highway that slipped like a conveyor belt beneath my front wheels. I leaned one arm out the window, letting the winds of Indiana whiplash my skin. Indiana: the word meant Indian country—or did it mean one single female Indian, deserted by her male, standing alone on a long prairie, searching the horizon for a friend? So many Indian wars on the prairie, so many buffalo chased and killed, so many pounds of human flesh, blood seeping into the black, rich ground, where later wheat and corn would wave! New people coming, innocent of the past like babies whose only sin is avarice for life, greed, murderous instincts, self-centered passion and a will to suck and grab in pure ferocity. We rushed by gas stations and snack bars, vegetable stands, and for a while the road curved along the railroad track and the freight cars whizzed past, clattering and whistling, drowning out all thought. A thousand cars long, steaming across the country. Orange, brown, and blue boxes on wheels, carrying sofas to La Jolla, grapefruit to Tucson and mail to Oregon.

"Sarah, look at the train, it lasts forever," I shouted. She didn't hear me. The roar of the wheels shut out my voice. Her head was down; rereading her comics, I supposed. "Sarah," I shouted again. The train howled in my ears. I tried to go faster to catch up with the engine, to wave at the engineer, but even at 85 or 90 mph, the cars pulled ahead, and the wind vibrations shook the station wagon like choppy waves hitting the sides of the little rowboat Alex and I used to fish in that last summer at the Cape. Once he was in the boat, his brown chest up to the sun, swilling from the bottle that never left his side, the bottle I no longer thought was romantic like a coonskin cap or a ski pole—now I saw it as a bottle, or a wall of bottles with Alex and me on opposite sides, and I couldn't get through or over the wall, but was forced to sit like a doomed Thisbe listening to words of love from an imagined Pyramus.

Once he looked at me as I was intently watching the gulls swoop down on their small prey. "Wouldn't you be better off," he said, "if you'd married a Jewish teacher, one who belonged to the union and did after school remedial work with retarded kids, and thought a little two-family house in Queens shared with his sister would be paradise? —Why didn't you get that kind of guy, Emily?" he asked.

"I really don't know," I said. "I guess I had ambitions."

"You're sweet," he laughed, and I felt happy for an hour or so.

WHAT IF a tire blew, what if I steered wrong, what if we crashed into the side of the train? Would we derail the freight or would we die, bones and gut on the roadside unnoticed by anyone till the state police came by, or a boy and girl from Greenwood or Plattsburg looking for a secret place to screw? Would they find any identification in the luggage? Who would they call?

I slowed the car to fifty, and then stopped entirely, letting the train go by till there was a distancing of noise and a sudden silence, the great silence that fills the air after a loud sound.

"I have to go to the bathroom," Sarah said, breaking into the emptiness that had seemed so vast I thought I had been swallowed by the sky.

"All right, next gas station," I said, and started the motor.

"No," said Sarah, "I mean I really have to go. Now!"

"Oh, come on," I said, "you can hold it a little."

"No, now, or I'll just have to go in the back of the car," and her face turned red, and the whine in her voice convinced me.

"For Christ's sake"—I pulled over into a field.

A farm house rose in the distance, some plow horses grazed ahead; the lettuces and the radishes, the beets and the beans, were planted in neat rows as far as the eye could see.

"All right, go ahead."

"Well, don't look," she said. "Turn around."

So I turned and looked at the road while Sarah squatted above the baby lettuce, fertilizing the earth.

"I need tissue," she said, and I dug some out of my pocketbook.

"It's not very clean," she complained.

"It's the best I can do," I replied.

When she had put her jeans back on, and we started again, I turned on the radio and we drove for an hour or so to the sounds of WPXR Indianapolis, John Shorty, the local disc jockey, interrupting the rock music every few minutes to tell us what was going to happen at the speedway next week, where to get bargain shoes that pinch neither the feet nor the pocketbook, where kids could get free lollipops with their haircuts, and what flavor mayonnaise he liked on his ham sandwiches. Between the hard-rock songs and soft-sell commercials, he placed phone calls to local listeners, asking them to identify a mystery song for a long honeymoon and five hundred dollars. No one got it. I began to suspect it wasn't a legitimate song at all, but rather crab sounds placed on tape by an undersea explorer.

"Those songs are all about drugs, for your information, Mother," Sarah said. I hadn't really been listening to the words, but I suppose she was right. "You're really not with it, are you?" she said.

"What do you know, what exactly have you found out about drugs?" I asked calmly.

"Nothing," she said. "We just talk about it in the fifth grade."

"What do you say?" I asked.

"We talk about the fast girls in the sixth grade who've tried it."

"Oh," I said, feeling helpless to protect my child from the monsters that gathered at the 72nd Street fountain, creatures that should be in the zoo, malformed dwarfs who will offer my daughter trips to faraway places from which she may never come back, and, like Ceres, I will be combing the earth, pleading with the gods to give me back my daughter, who will have gone to fuck with death a million miles under the earth's crust.

We were entering Wabash country, nearing Terre Haute, nearing Illinois. We passed coal mines and clay quarries, a few paint factories and a thickening of houses, a narrowing of highways. The city lay ahead. I started to look for a motel with a swimming pool. Rest Your Head, Duck Inn, Howard's Hole, were all rejected, partly because I was driving too fast. A momentum had caught me, it seemed as if I and the other cars on the road were flying down a mail chute, propelled by vacuum and gravity to a destination at the bottom. I felt a kind of release, as if I were a shooting star arching through the night, never thinking of the time I would fizzle, burn out, dissolve into chemical gas.

I finally stopped at the Wabash Basin Motel, a little outside Terre Haute. Its clear turquoise pool and orange chairs attracted Sarah's eye, and she soon was splashing away, calling to me to look at each fishlike maneuver she made. I thought of other waters as I saw her in the pool. I thought of her father's hands as he held her above the waves. . . . The motel manager noticed my bruised shins and face and asked me if the car had been in an accident. I told him no, I had merely fallen in a careless moment. He looked at me suspiciously, as if I had no right to stumble. If I were a proper person, I would always glide about gracefully and never mark myself with blood or pain.

I thought of friends. I had not spoken to anyone since several weeks before we left New York. I had not wanted to answer questions. I had not wanted to tell lies. I had not wanted to tell anyone the truth. I would have told my grandmother, but she had died of deterioration, of urine blockage and fat tissues around the heart many years ago. Did I have friends? Or were they social connections in the art world—people pleased to know the artist, to own his work; other artists, tolerant of each other, knowing that the other, the not-me, was seen only through the telescope, turned round, and that dot on the distant horizon was a friend's face peering into yours?

Artists' wives and girlfriends understand each other better than they will admit. Each with an obsession, a vicarious sense of creation, a love of power reflected on them, not personally earned, but any good day they can be caught basking in the reflected warm glow. They protect their mates, they order the canvas and the paint, they cart babies in sacks from one loft to another. They mother, worship, perform strange acts in the dark, dressed in odd clothes to please fetishists whose distorted inner eyes demand peculiar things—but they carefully hide their own souls under the mantle of service for their menfolk, and by constant caring, carrying drinks, soothing rough moments, they earn the right to travel by the side of a creator, a painter of form, shape and design, a godhead to a female whose own hands have frozen like ice mountains, and whose brain despises its own tormented small capacities. Some of these women were our friends, but I could not count on them to call me once I had been severed from my head; and Alex, who always was available for daytime meetings and late-night activities, would now be more than ever prey. And I, like yesterday's cottage cheese, can be forgotten—an orgy of eating begun.

I think, here I am outside the city limits of Terre Haute, and I know no one and may never make a human connection again—no man may ever love my special movements, heat rising in his sexual glands for me—I may hang alone like a marionette whose strings have become too tangled to play with any more. The thought frightens me—I feel cold and empty, a breast-beating heroine, my God, from the worst of daytime television. For a while I bask in self-pity like a hippo in the mud. I go away from the pool and put on a shirt to cover myself. The brooding will not do—we must go and visit something.

"Sarah, come out of the pool. We have to see the city—we have to learn something to make this long trip worthwhile."

I bribe Sarah with the promise of some new comics and an ice cream cone.

My grandfather had always wanted to visit Terre Haute because it was the birthplace of his great hero, Eugene V. Debs. My grandfather told me often of the martyrdom of the leader of the Socialist party, the man who started shoveling coal in the trains. He moved across the West talking to people, and ended by declaring an ideal for his country, so beautiful and good, so hopeful and pure, he could only be jailed and defeated and destroyed. Whenever my grandfather would speak of him, his eyes would fill with tears, and I would know they were tears for me because Eugene V. Debs had been killed before I could know him.

My grandfather, whose small accountancy business had prospered in the Upper Bronx, never forgot his boyhood dream of revolution—of pamphlets and books hidden from the police in pigpens and chicken coops. He identified not just with the Jewish workers the world over, but with Indians trying to get free of colonial overlords, with strikers in Detroit and miners in Kentucky and deafmutes and cerebral palsy victims and "colored," and farmers whose mortgages were foreclosed by the bank. He mourned over flood victims and anarchists, and each night after dinner he read all the newspapers including the *Jewish Forward*, moaning and groaning over the disasters that daily struck the little people, the working class, the ones without power or money or arms to rectify the endless injustices, the calamities, forced on them by man and God. He was just not the type to take up a gun, to engage in guerrilla warfare, labor organizing or bomb throwing, so each day he went on the subway and traveled to his office, where he helped businessmen to prosper and keep track of their prospering.

Sometimes his heart ached with such a real pain he thought he was dying. A taxi would pull up in front of our building; my grandfather's associate and a young clerk would carry and drag him up the many stairs. My grandmother would weep and scream and call the doctor, and my grandfather would gasp and choke and pant, his skin an ashen gray.

"The pain in my heart," he would say—"Emily, Emily, hold my hand," and I would hold his hand and stroke his arm.

"Please, please let it be all right," I would say silently.

The doctor would come, and he would listen to the heart, and he would say, "I don't think anything is really wrong—just some rest and aspirin."

And we would tiptoe around, and then, a day or so later, my grandfather would be up and dressed. "My heart is fine today," he would say, "and there's nothing to worry about" —and off he would go till the next attack.

And so we came to expect the taxi and the panting and the heaving and the doctor coming and going, and it became more ceremonial with each attack; more and more formally did my grandmother scream and cry; more and more routinely did I hold his hand; and yet the drama never seemed to run its course, but played over and over through the years. All tests showed a strong constitution unaffected by either arteriosclerosis or coronary contractions, thrombosis or angina. Diagnostically it could only be too much sympathy with the underdog, too much guilt for not actively fighting on their behalf, too much sadness for one man to contain in a heart whose infinite capacity for pity pinched him till it hurt.

Eugene Debs was his idol, and on Sunday mornings, we would walk through Van Cortlandt Park, and he would tell me stories of strikes and strikebreakers, of the union shop and the bastards who finally put Debs in jail, proving free speech is an illusion—you can only disagree if no one listens. We bought pretzels and chestnuts from a vendor at the 242nd Street subway stop, and fed the squirrels stale bread and unwanted candy from the jar my grandmother kept on a high shelf.

Despite the fact my grandfather described the world as a vale of tears, a pisspot for the rich, an alligator swamp, a lion's den, a witch's cauldron, a catacomb without exit, we were not lonely or unhappy, my grandfather and I. We wailed at the wailing wall together and ate hot dogs with sauerkraut and mustard at a little store on Upper Broadway. My grandmother tried to keep the house kosher, tried to keep going to shul, in memory of the memories of her childhood and her parents across the ocean, forgotten, their names never mentioned in the New World. She tried to be respectable because respectability kept away the chaos that sometimes overwhelmed her, causing her to call out in her sleep, screaming wild sounds, a warning to the future, a mourning for the past.

My grandfather bought bacon from downtown and cooked it in all our frying pans; the smell would waft through the apartment house, while my grandmother silently suffered the stares of neighbors and the sense of wide-open emptiness that follows intense frustration. I understood my grandfather. Years of learning lessons in crude Russian shuls, years of being barefoot and cold, years of being a stranger wherever he went, had made of my grandfather a man who could never have led his people across the Red Sea—forty years in the desert. The leader had to be raised in a palace by the King's daughter, had to think of himself as a prince. A leader could not be defeated before he was four years old by harsh toilet training, too little food, and large Russian snowdrifts.

My grandfather was fit only to dream on the revolution, Eugene Debs' revolution, and in good moments when his blood ran high, he brought bacon into the house and dared his wife to raise her voice or harm the head he knew she loved.

Now in Terre Haute I decided to visit the birthplace of Debs—his name itself sounded like something one owed, a debit, an insufficiency, something on the negative side, debilitating, depleting. The American Promised Land took its socialist leader, its stoker of coals, and put him in jail, what else? As we drove into Terre Haute proper, past the Rotary Center, the Lions, the Elks Club, the banks, Greek-columned and large, the city center, the court house, the shoppers' mall, the movie house, I felt old hurts awakened.

I started to tell Sarah about Eugene Debs and the Locomotive Union where it all had started in the 1880's.

"Was he killed," Sarah asked, "like Martin Luther King and the Kennedys?"

"No, but he was in jail."

"Jail," she said, "that's nothing. Joan Baez's husband's been in jail. Wasn't he important enough to get shot?" she asked.

I tried again to tell her about the idea of the working man, the poor man sharing in the profits, the goods of the society.

She interrupted me. "Daddy isn't interested in politics," she said. "He says it's the same no matter what happens."

"Yes," I said, "that's what he thinks."

"How many comics can I buy?" she asked.

I drove to a little house on a tree-lined side street called Trade Street. An unimposing brick house, No. 25, had on it a gold plaque, telling us that Eugene V. Debs, 1855–

1926, was born and raised here. I looked around—philodendrons in the yard, red and white roses on a carefully painted trellis. It wasn't a terrible place to grow up, but it wasn't the pharaoh's palace either, and I wondered what had made Debs so special—a gift with words, of course, but Hitler had that too. I lifted Sarah up so she could look in the window of the little house. She said nothing. Shrines are never as effective as one hopes—they are just dead places that once held sacred objects or housed sacred persons, they are picked-over carcasses that do not satisfy the hungry traveler.

The neighborhood was still working class. The yards had swing sets and bicycles. The street was quiet, but I heard the whistle of the train from the tracks not far away. Sarah and I walked to the corner to find a store to buy ice cream and comics. On the way I calculated the number of refrigerators, television sets, cars and sofas that were bought on time in the houses we passed. If I knew the payments of each, I could find the absolute debt figure of the block. I imagined a hump of dollars attached to the backs of the adults. They walked around bearing their shiny appliances, weighted down with monthly payments, their spines bending from the burden, acquisitions increasing their appetite for more and more till the vertebrae cracked and crumbled, leaving the men and women crawling on their bellies, collecting crumbs from the floor with eager tongues and eyes that could now reach no higher than the scabby knee of a small child.

I found a little store with newspapers out front, a soda fountain, a comic-book rack and a drug section with all the cosmetics lined up for choice; like hookers on Eighth Avenue, most of the boxes had been on display too long, and the shine, the hard gleaming edge, was off. The man behind the counter, a little, old and rumpled European with a foreign accent, came over and asked if he could help us. He fixed ice cream cones for us, and Sarah went off to the comics rack to make her selection.

"Are you strangers?" he said.

"Yes," I answered, "we're traveling across the country."

He looked at me intently. "Have you no home?"

"Well," I hesitated, "we live in New York now. Everything is temporary with us." I wanted him to talk to me—a familiar kind of face, worn out with its own thoughts. "Where are you from?" I asked.

"Berlin," he answered, "a long time ago—then Montreal, Rochester, North Carolina, Arkansas, Oregon, and now Terre Haute. I move a lot because," he leaned over the counter to whisper so Sarah wouldn't hear, "I'm running away from my ghost, my shadow; it follows me—I change my name, I change my business, and it stays at my elbow all the time."

Ah, my new friend was a lunatic—state institutions must have seen him come and go. I wanted to leave his little store; let him be haunted without my involvement. Many times I've seen drunks weaving down the Bowery streets, twitching, leaning on lampposts and cars, and I've always wanted to run, to turn away, as if their demons would rush at my throat and choke me till I lay limp on the sidewalk. I am at once guilty of the other's condition and a possible victim of his irrational rage.

"Is it a European ghost?" I said. "Are you Jewish?"

"Yes," he said.

"I am too," I told him, and silently we shared a vision

of boxcars carrying the dead and the living off into a night so dark it cannot be remembered or believed.

"But," he said, "my ghost is no Nazi, no victim of the Reich, he is my brother."

"What?" I asked.

"I was well-born, the son of a doctor and his wealthy wife. My mother stained blood nine months and stayed in bed, hoping to save the baby—and thus we were born, my brother and I, and the midwife screamed, and my mother, weak, wept as though she saw the future. We were attached, my brother and I, spine to spine, hip to hip—two heads, two mouths, two brains, but not quite two bodies. One liver, one spleen, two stomachs, two hearts, two circulatory systems, but one liver and one spleen. 'Kill them, kill them,' screamed my mother. But my father said, 'No, one will live, the other will die. We will separate them. One will live and one will die.' By cruel accident I had the liver and spleen in my part of the unit that was us, and I was chosen to live, and my brother severed from me on the operating table. He breathed some days till his system filled with poison and he died, while I gained and grew only a raw scar to show that I had been attached to another—that I was myself and someone else, a brother who could only live if his body melded into mine. But then at night—at first only at night in my early years—I could feel my brother's spirit hovering over me, dying to get in, to displace me, to possess my body and take it for his own. I could feel him trying to open my mouth, his little hands prying at my lips to slide through my nostrils, to ease up my anus, to take over and throw me into the small grave that had been his. Later he would try during the day, and for the last fifteen years I have guarded myself against him at all times. I hardly sleep, but I am vigilant and I can live many years yet."

Sarah came over with her comics, more adventures of Archie, Veronica and a villain named Jughead. I wished the drugstore owner well. I was happy to leave him and his ghost to do battle together. I thought of the unlucky one, the baby without the liver—did he have a great musical talent to compensate, was he the clever one, the sweet one? Did the one with the spleen have a chink in his brain at birth or was his madness simple guilt?

Didn't he know everyone's life has been stolen from someone else? If the seed and the sperm had not met at that exact split second, another sperm would have entered a moment later, and another whole different person would be born in place of the first. Everybody's life precludes someone else's. That is the basic premise of birth, and the killer instinct in man lies in this original sin, on his doing away with, having beat out, all the other souls that might have been, that withered in the battlefield of the mother's vagina, as he or she triumphantly divides and grows within the now sealed-off, protected uterus.

We walked back toward the car, parked in front of Debs' house, Sarah holding tight to her comics as once she'd clutched a faded pink blanket and a fuzzy dog. Anyone who's taken care of a baby knows how real is the terror of loneliness, the fright of being helpless, abandoned like a bug on its back, frantically waving its fragile legs; unable to right itself, unable to eat, drink, move forward or backward, it can only wait for death either in gradual pain of starvation or the instant crushing demolition of an enemy's beak or foot, squashing the last hopes to nothing.

I remembered Sarah crying in the crib, crying to be

picked up, reassured, touched by another human. What if I had wandered off, never returned, left her there, screaming until exhaustion took over and then death? . . . A terror, a primeval dark terror, came over me as we walked on the street. I forced myself to pay attention to the houses, cars, and people. I noticed the American flag hanging out on poles or ropes on many of the porches. Those flags said clearly, "We are white, we want law and order, we want to keep our turf for ourselves. We don't mind killing Asians. We are proud to be Americans. We don't intend to open up our unions or our bowling alleys or our parks to strangers. We haven't got enough as it is. We work too hard for nothing. God Bless America." Debs' people, railroad workers—it made me sad they didn't want to share with others.

My grandfather would have been confused. The victims turn exploiters, given a quarter of a chance—the little man buys himself big boots with his first dollars in order to step on someone else. My grandfather would never have understood. A thousand years of history had made it impossible for him to be the aggressor, to do the stamping and crating of bodies, to lean or push on others. His genes had learned to cry, his muscles had weakened, his eyes saw always from the bottom looking up at the raised fist ready to come down.

We got into the car, and Sarah, reading her comics, seemed content. I decided to drive around Terre Haute, perhaps find the reconstructed pioneer kitchen that was housed in one of the local museums. I turned down a few streets, took a left and a right, moving aimlessly in the direction of the green lights. I noticed the buildings getting shabbier, the electric signs brighter, the porches with broken steps, paint peeling, windows broken and chalk writing, billboards on all the walls, garbage cans turned over, broken bottles on the sidewalk. The section was black. Black faces showed out windows, black children played ball on the street, and heat of summer weighed heavy and gray.

I turned again left a block, right a block, and we were deeper still into the black section of town. I began to feel afraid, because I didn't know how to get out—afraid, I reassured myself, of nothing, of other human beings going about their normal day. I despised myself for feeling strange, for the nagging worry I couldn't lose. At a red light I locked the car doors, watching the men nodding on the steps watching me with half-open, dulled eyes. Burn, Baby, Burn. I could understand—if it were mine, I would be the first to take a torch. The flat, charred land could be no worse.

But where was I? I stopped to take out a city map and figure out how to get back to the motel, its orange canvas beach chairs looking more inviting each moment. I couldn't read it—the spiderweb of lines and numbers only confused me further. I couldn't even find Apple Street, the last sign I'd seen, on the map. At the corner was a grocery store. I decided to get out and ask a human question (where am I?)—to ask another human. I opened the door, cautioning Sarah to stay in the car. She didn't look up. I walked to the corner, feeling all eyes on me, a woman lost, a lost woman, an alien—I am not what you think, I am a refugee international socialist failure. I am not responsible for anything. Am I not responsible? I could feel the stares on the back of my legs, on my hips. The children stopped playing and ran into doorways. I'm not the welfare inspector, I'm not a school teacher. I'm just one lost lady. I flapped my map around, hoping that would explain me. I held tight to my purse. By nature, by upbringing, I am of the oppressed, not of the oppressors, but that doesn't show in my color, in my clothes, in my car.

Somebody kicked a beer can, and in the silence around me the sounds vibrated like so many accusing tongues: "Your fault, your fault." "Why my fault?" "Because you didn't do enough. You went on living your private life, you thought your husband's paintings were important, that color and aesthetic mattered when babies were hungry, when families couldn't even afford to buy food stamps. When black was down, you lived in clean houses in white sections where the garbage was collected daily, and the police never stopped you for loitering when you went window-shopping downtown. What have you done about it? Wailing at dinner parties doesn't count a damn. What have you done about it? Your kid in some snooty school that uses the latest in teaching devices, small classes, sweet kids—what have you done for the others?"

I walked toward the store—pale face, pale soul, no guts, no give, a rigid, tight-assed, bleached-out, cop-out, fink-out, washout—but what to do about myself?

"Lady!" a voice said from behind. I stopped. My hands trembled. "Lady."

White teeth flashed, a porkpie hat appeared, a pink wet vinyl shirt unzippered to the waist—a pimp recruiting me? A pusher peddling, a purse thief ready for the snatch, a rapist about to invite me into a back-alley? An earthquake has come, split the country; black and white on either side of a terrible divide: one either works for the revolution, for the just turnabout of events, slave into master, master into slave, or one sits holding a gun, a policeman's billy club, protecting property—no shades of gray possible, just the cracked earth and the tremors that shake the ground again and again.

"Lady," insisted the voice.

"Yes," I answered, my knees trembling.

"You wanta buy some photographs—black men showing off their natural powers—five bucks a set?"

I didn't really want to see it. I'd fallen for this before—why should I do it again? I could imagine for myself long, erect black penises threatening me with their black power. I was more alarmed than excited by the idea, but I felt it was not wise to refuse the glistening young man whose pockets bulged with what I imagined were zip knives and blackjacks. I took the money out of my purse, and he handed me an envelope—at least the exchange was honest in good capitalist tradition. I felt somehow reassured. There is a brotherhood in buying and selling. I looked back. Sarah was playing jacks in the car; a host of small black children pressed against the window, watching her fancy fingerwork. I asked my pornographer how to get downtown, center of Terre Haute. He shrugged as if he'd never been there and walked off around the corner.

I tried to enter the grocery store, but four teen-aged boys blocked my way. I decided to ask them how to get downtown. One kept staring at my purse, another at my breasts. No one spoke. I had sent money to SNCC and CORE, to Coretta King and Charles Evers, to Roy Wilkins, Biafra, Pakistan, Angela Davis, Bobby Seale. I was not entirely guilty of indifference, and yet the smells of my life had been such that I knew now I was guilty of French restaurants, and trips to Italy, weekends in Connecticut, an education that included Mozart and Henry

Miller, a home that had never had a toilet unflushed. An occasional cockroach was the only wildlife my grandmother ever met; drugs meant aspirin and antibiotics to me, and the future was always open. That I had closed myself in a studio with a man who didn't see me was my own fault, not a social crime at all.

"My child is waiting in the car," I said, hoping to appeal to chivalrous instincts. I covered my breasts with my purse, hoping to look sexless if not poor. A transistor radio blared loud rock as, realizing I could not get into the store, I turned around to get back to the car. The boys moved forward. I was deciding whether it would be better to run for the car or walk coolly, slowly, as if I were not terrified. I heard a siren, a screech of brakes, and a police car appeared. The door opened, and two big red-necked, pink-cheeked, heavy policemen stood before me. Behind me the boys melted away, like memories of last night's quarrel forgiven in the morning sun. I was saved. My friend the policeman!

"You all right, lady?" one said.

"Oh, yes, just lost," I replied.

"What were you doing here? This pigpen is no place for you."

"Well, I was lost," I explained, showing him my car and Sarah.

"You have a child with you? You must be crazy to come here."

"Well, I got lost," I explained again.

The street was silent, almost empty. The enemy occupation troops had come. I was caught between the angry mob and the Gestapo, and I needed the Gestapo to escape. The SS were on my side. I smiled at them warmly—brutes, bullies, tyrants, whose badge and color gave them a cruel superiority. I hated them, prison guards and detectives and patrolmen, hunters of small rabbits and little pheasants, spoilers of nests, trappers of tiny wild furry things—chains and guns and spikes. They threw their weight around, and yet I was so profoundly glad to see them.

"Officers, show me the way to downtown Terre Haute," I begged, and they obliged, escorting me back to the motel where, exhausted, I lay down on the single bed, listening to Sarah splashing in the pool outside.

A wandering Jewess gets very tired. I took a cigarette, poisoning myself slowly with nicotine. I was at least contributing to the employment of the tobacco farmers whose ringwormed children needed care. I reached into my purse and withdrew the envelope I had bought. It smelled of Dentyne chewing gum or hairspray or shoe polish. I opened the envelope eagerly; now in the safety of my locked hotel room, I could appreciate a good sexual display. I spread the photographs out before me. They were pictures cut out from a magazine, each one of a different make of car, shiny chrome, big wheels and new paint job showing the body off to its best advantage. Cars! I had been had again. Five dollars' worth of Detroit's wet dreams. I felt fearful. Would I ever be able to ford the future?

THE NEXT DAY we started out again. Now I was determined to visit a reservation. We had seen enough of motels, highways, gas stations. And now I wanted to go off the concrete strips, onto the side roads, into the country, to find an Indian's crazy language like that of the Finns, a people a universe away from Jews who easily catch colds in small drafts, believe in majesty as revealed in the fine print of their books. Jews could never have seen the face of God in rustling leaves or animal footprints, in moonshine or harvest fruit. The Hassidic Jews talked about it —but they talked too much—I just don't believe they ever saw anything. Jews have always sat in dingy closets explaining the mysteries, ordering and commenting on the supernatural through elaborate legislation of the daily labors. The result is a capacity for science, making lists of ingredients to go into test tubes, and watching the connection and effect of the invisible chemicals. The result has been centuries of violinists and cellists, scientists and social workers, knocking against each other—but few surf-riders, sun worshippers, mountain climbers, modern dancers, cowboys or sky-divers. Most Jewish women are twice deprived. They don't run naked in the woods following the wild spirits of nature, and they don't get to share in the legal Talmudic store; so they remain ignorant and empty, creatures bound, knotted up by rules without reason, their intelligence like wax candles dripping on the carefully polished table until nothing remains.

Sarah is now looking forward to getting to the reservation. She had told her friends that she would bring them souvenirs, and often in the last days she had reminded me that I had promised we could buy them something when we got there.

Like the French Romantics of the eighteenth century, I was suffering from a noble-savage syndrome—everything primitive seemed to me beautiful, civilization with its electric pencil sharpeners and ice trays a despoiler. Alex had particularly fixed his mind on primitive art: large heads with protruding lips, masks with eyebrows that writhed like snakes across the face, small pots with broken handles and animal cartoons etched in sharp lines: "That's what I am," he'd say with pride, "a brother of a barbarian craftsman, hammering simple designs, finding terror in bold angles and firm colors."

When I was at Hunter College, majoring in early childhood education (so, my grandmother said, that I could always earn a living no matter what, receive health insurance, a pension and decent social security), a girlfriend of mine who painted tableaux of nude women on silk screens invited me to a party in the Village. That night I wore my mother's earrings and black stockings; the determination I felt to break away from my planned future and enter like a Hollywood starlet into new orbits must have showed in the set of my jaw or the bend of my back, because Alex came over, introduced himself and said he would do my portrait on a cocktail napkin. He took a piece of charcoal from his jeans pocket and drew a black cross. From either end of the T-bar hung gold earrings—it was me, exactly me, and in my enthusiasm, I instantly allowed my spirit to leave my body so I could devote myself to tending the love that rushed in to fill the cavity where my private, single soul had formerly been.

In the early years when we always went to museums and galleries together I would stand quietly beside him, trying to see what his eyes saw. He was always looking for the reductions to basic elements. He asked me once, "Do you remember when you were a child and learned to recognize circle, triangle and rectangle?" I didn't remember, but he did. His parents, socialites, débris of the Fitzgerald era, had a large estate in Princeton, and he remembered that he was there on the patio having tea, when his nanny told him the important words; circle, triangle, rectangle, he said that was the only thing he ever learned that had mattered, that changed things. I couldn't understand, but I pretended to—I tried hard to forget the illusion that I was the man I loved.

Later years, after Sarah was born, he went by himself looking for his visual necessities. I stayed home, walking about his studio, wondering where the dybbuk was sleeping, hiding the spirit that had been Emily Brimberg, the child and young woman, Emily who had owned at least a name to give her continuity, who had taken a certain pleasure in things. Emily Brimberg had disappeared into the crevices of the apartment or under the oriental rug we had received from Alex's parents as a wedding present. Was the dybbuk ever going to come back to give me back to myself, I would wonder.

In the last months before Alex finally packed all his bags and we acknowledged to each other we had at last unraveled our love, I got a call from Michael Forzhamer: Would I meet him for lunch? I was delighted to hear his voice—my childhood sweetheart, my first boyfriend, the boy next door. Even better; he had lived in the J line of apartments in the very same building I lived in. As children we had played together in the laundry room while his mother and my grandmother told lurid tales in a Yiddish they presumed we didn't understand. When it snowed, we bumped down the mountain steps of the building to the street below and threw snowballs at passing cars. He could always make me cry by saying boys were better than girls—they could throw better, make more money, pick up heavier things and were smarter. Once he said that, and later I pretended I was going to kiss him and instead bit him on the cheek. Drops of blood fell on his polo shirt, and he screamed and screamed, and we weren't friends for a long time after that.

Michael was always good-looking—round and soft like mashed potatoes. His deep brown eyes were round like manhole covers on the city street. His mother watched him all the time—"Don't get dirty, now, Michael, watch those hands; don't play with the dirty stick, Michael, it might hurt your hands." His hands had early learned to pick up the cello bow, and no matter what was happening on the street, at four thirty every day he went in to practice, holding the smooth wood of the cello body between his pudgy thighs, bending his curly head over the sheets of music. He would rock on his padded bottom, and the sounds would fly into the air, mellow and deep, like a bearded old man crying because nothing is forever. I would sit and listen, patient with the starting and the stopping. He became a part of me after years of walking to school together, of dirty jokes (Q: What hops from bed to bed and is green with bumps on it? A: A prostitoad) and stealing candy bars. Like my own hands or arms—I hardly thought of him as separate, or as Michael, but as my reflection in a mirror, familiar, unattended, not respected, but not despised.

Later, in the seventh grade, we started having parties, and I always went with Michael because it was easy. I had my thoughts on more dashing types: Philip Schwartz, whose eyelids drooped mysteriously over his sad eyes and who claimed his grandfather who was a Rabbi could make their kitchen table rise four feet into the air at his command; Seymour Green, who was the biggest among us, and blond—he was always the head of the Gestapo, marching around and giving orders as we were herded to our death in the shower in a game none of us liked, but we couldn't stop playing nevertheless. I remember us standing in the Forzhamer bathtub, six of us, the plastic shower curtain with orange flowers printed on it shielding us from view, as we choked and screamed till the last one had fallen on the pile at the bottom of the bathtub extermination camp. Warm, pressed against each other, we would giggle and squirm and perspire in our clothes till somehow the game ended.

Michael and I had petted when the lights went out; we French-kissed, and he put his white doughy hands on my little pretensions of breasts that poked hopefully through the threads of my pink angora sweater. I always felt I was practicing with Michael for the time when Philip or Seymour or someone else would see the truth and find me irresistible. We went for walks after school, to the free concerts in Van Cortlandt Park. I thought Michael was like my childhood bottle, like the warm milk my grandmother tested on her wrist. Someday I'd do without him.

Once at Lucy's party I felt him hot and heavy on me, his tongue pushing at my lips and his hands under my skirt. My God, I thought, I have to get away. He won't respect me if I let him do this. He won't like me any more if he thinks I'm a fast girl. My reputation would be finished, and he'd tell everybody, and I'd never be loved at all. I was so concerned with all the repercussions of my lost reputation that I couldn't feel any sex myself, though the dampness in my pants told me I was not a block of wood. I pushed him away, off the chair; in the dim light cast by Mrs. Dolger's hall lamp, I saw the other couples rolling about on the floor. I saw my girlfriends pushing and pulling, defending their virtue while trying not to offend their boyfriends—a delicate balance. I went home and wouldn't go out with Michael any more. We saw each other—often we talked a lot; he went to Music and Art High School and I went with him to a dance or two there, but I was so cold he never touched me again, and when he started taking Marilyn Begner out, I felt a contempt for both of them. She was dumb and probably good enough for him. As for me, I started to plan for the extinction of the Jewish race —breed it out, fall in love with the enemy—a thought so wicked that I would hug myself with excitement and pleasure each time it crossed my mind.

"No one wants someone else's chewed gum," and with that warning my grandmother would threaten me with a life of enforced chastity, spinsterhood and disgrace if I allowed anyone but my husband into my treasure—an expression I correctly understood not as a euphemism, but as an accurate description of the total capital on which I was to build my fortune.

Michael Forzhamer—I hadn't seen him since the summer before he went to Oberlin with a full music scholarship. We had met and talked on the subway platform. I was waiting for the subway to take me to work, my summer file-clerk's job at Merrill Lynch, and he was waiting for the subway to take him to the music school where he was teaching children the rudiments of cello. I don't remember what we talked about—old friends, college plans—but as I looked at him, I was thinking, I don't want a man like that, a man who plays Scarlatti and whose mother washes out his underwear each night. I want a cowboy, lean and hard, with beady eyes and muscles that ripple beneath his tattered shirt, a guy who's used a hammer and nails, and a fist.

I met Michael Forzhamer for lunch at a little restaurant in the neighborhood. He was now a concert performer, a teacher, and, he told me, in analysis with a Dr. Stone whose office was right around the corner.

"I had to see you again, Emily," he said.

I felt a surge of love: my darling Michael, so many years I've not seen him, a part of myself, a childhood of bubblegum and Wonder Woman comics, of Captain Marvel and the Green Hornet, of Brahms and Mozart. And I remembered his barmitzvah, when he gave me a corsage, and I sat next to him at the center table, and everyone said we were so sweet together. "Michael . . ." I wanted to apologize for my desire to breed out the Jewish race, I wanted to explain to him how it had seemed that so much unnecessary suffering could be spared if the victims would just join the enemy and give up their ancient superstitions.

I was just about to reach across the table and touch our childhood, hold it tenderly for a moment before returning it to the rush of time, when he said, "You were really a bitch. I mean I want to tell you you're probably the bitchiest woman around. You started early, a sex tease, an icebox that knew just how to devastate—Right, bitch? Let me drink to you." And on he went. Dr. Stone had really showed him what I had been up to all those years, teasing him, allowing him to love me, and then always putting my foot in his face; talking to him about other guys, about moving away, pretending not to know his lust was high, his love was intense. He reminded me. Once he had come to visit me in my junior year of high school, and I was in the shower washing my hair for a date; I invited him in as if he were not a male, as if he didn't count. I let him watch me shower, and he thought his skin would burst from lust and shame—and I kept talking about nothing, as if I weren't torturing him.

"Why, Emily? Why did you do it?"

I tried to remember. I didn't know he loved me? I didn't know his hands hid an erect penis, throbbing and thrashing around like a trapped bird in the wool of his trousers? I didn't think. I apologized.

"Too late for apologies now, Emily," he said. "I remembered you differently," he said. "You look kinda worn out." And he paid the check and left.

"Guilt to you, too, Michael Forzhamer!" I shouted down the street after him, and people looked at me oddly. . . .

WE DROVE on Route 70 for one hundred miles, a peaceful silence in the car, Sarah looking out the back window at the landscape we had passed through, and I looking ahead at the scene we were approaching. I left the highway at exit 40, following the map I had received at a gas station a few miles back. I wanted to go to the Indian country, not just so Sarah could bring back souvenirs, but for myself, to confirm that Indians were not the scalping, war-whooping barbarians of the movies we used to see on Saturday afternoons.

As we were driving along, a mass of Technicolor film strips filtered through the memory. The Loew's at 184th Street was almost dark-blue with a starlit domed canopy and, glittering overhead, golden Buddhas decorating the upper balcony—a true house of mystery a billion children dreamed together of burning fire, horses writhing on the ground, arrows piercing the sides of covered wagons, their wheels turning helplessly in the dust. Feathered, painted savages carrying off little children into the hills—a generation saw it together. Wagons forming protective circles, poke bonnets blowing in the wind, rag dolls abandoned to the coyotes. We saw the cavalry, blue-coated, high-booted, tall and strong Americans, come over the hills, tight-lipped, determined, bravely riding through canyons and rapid rivers flooded by spring thaws, coming to rescue the hero, the heroine, and kill by the hundred thousands the Indians, furred and feathered brown bodies dropping in pools of blood as the triumphant music swelled in the background. As the lights came on, we searched under the seats for dropped gloves, scarves and lost pieces of buttery popcorn.

Sophomore year I took Professor Browning's Anthropology 204; then there followed years of reading the real story, the other side. But nothing could erase the early images that sat in my head like so many contradictory thoughts, causing loss of equilibrium, lack of certainty. Now we would see the real Indian, denatured of course, but still not a cigar-store statue, a genuine relative of the old Sioux gathered on the highlands of Oklahoma, outsiders, minorities, leftouts, people I could feel identified with. Didn't the Baal Shem Tov tell the Jewish people in the eighteenth century to go dance in the streets, to worship God with joy, to sing in the face of danger and death, to free their souls, to dance with God? Unfortunately the followers of the Baal Shem Tov made up a lot of rules about how to be joyous, what clothes to wear, how and on what days to open your heart, and the system became a rope around the neck of the young Hassidim who survive these days only out of stubbornness, out of a great obstinacy very like that of the dark-eyed Indian whose memories include Walter Winchell, Fibber McGee and Molly, Uncle Don, the squeaking door of The Inner Sanctum, and Doctor Christian healing the warts of WASP Americans, as well as the tom-tom, the Shaman's ritual night, and the tales of heroes and animals grandmothers struggled to remember and repeat.

We drove for miles more. Sarah started to play jacks again. I looked at the corn and the farms and the small towns that were no more than a post office, a bank and a cluster of stores. We saw boys on tractors, spotted dogs running along the roadside. The back of my neck got tired and ached. My arms were stiff from holding the wheel so long. I couldn't find a motel or a hotel to stop in, so I kept pushing on. There was a diner outside of Plattsburg, and we stopped for supper.

"I want a motel," said Sarah. "I don't care if it doesn't have a swimming pool as long as it's air-conditioned and has a TV."

"Where can we spend the night?" I asked the young waitress who brought us our frozen pizzas and root beers. "We are going to the reservation," I added conversationally.

"There's a nice inn," she said, "twenty-five miles down the road." I decided we'd try to make it, although I was suddenly so tired I thought maybe we'd just sleep in the car.

We started driving. It got dark slowly, the shadows turning black and the lights coming on in the distant farm houses. The road was very narrow; trucks speeded past. We drove by a church that was having a meeting or a party or a wedding, overheard music in the wind for a second or two. It seemed, as it got dark, that we alone were without place or known destination. I was so tired. My back ached with a pain that started in my shoulders and went down to my hips. It seemed I had been driving for days and days. The muscles in my legs cramped. I was afraid I would fall asleep for even a moment or two and crash the car into a tree or into a boulder lying on the side of the road, or a car coming the other way with refreshments for the church party.

The stars were out in the sky. I could see the Milky Way; light years separated me from home, wherever it was. I pulled the car over off the road into a grassy field. I hoped it was wild growth, not someone's plantings. My tires sunk in the soft earth and I stopped the motor.

"Sarah, we're sleeping here," I said.

"We can't," she said, "I have to brush my teeth."

"Tonight you can skip it," I replied.

"But what about bears or rapists?" she asked.

"Well, I'll lock the doors."

"We'll get monoxide poisoning," she whimpered.

"I'll open the windows a little. I just can't drive any more." I nearly cried.

"I don't know why," she said. "Why didn't we take an

airplane like other divorcing people? Hedwig's mother flew down and back and was divorced over the weekend. It didn't have to be such a production. I'm probably going to get a cavity tonight," she complained, as I lay down on the front seat of the car, pulling my sweater over me, feeling the seat leather still warm from a day of the sun. I thought as I fell asleep that if the Lord sent angels down to wrestle all night with women, he might send one down to me—because I needed an angel, even a fighting angel, in this far Oklahoma field.

When I woke, it was dark. First I heard the sounds of a heavy falling rain on the car roof, and then I saw the water washing over the windshield. I heard the wind turning the leaves of a nearby tree inside out. I saw the sky split by lightning and heard the thunder deep in the belly of a nearby valley moving closer to the car. The flashes of lightning lit up the field in front of us like the rays of an atomic explosion brilliant across the sad Pacific. I felt cold and damp. I looked back at Sarah sleeping on our beach blanket. I hoped she would wake and need to sit near me, need me to put my arms around her and draw magic circles of safety, but she slept on, turning, stirring with the claps of thunder, but never really waking. Once she sat up and said to me, "Turn off the TV, I'm trying to sleep," and down again she went into her blanket, dreaming perhaps of the thousand cartoons she had watched in her small lifetime—of Elmer Fudd shooting Bugs Bunny full of buckshot, of Bugs Bunny catching Elmer Fudd's foot in a bear trap, of Felix the Cat with a bag of tricks to make Swiss cheese out of burglar mice, of Astroboy smashing wicked scientists into the outer galaxies, of Casper the Friendly Ghost scaring an old man into paroxysms of breathlessness, of Good triumphing over Bad in endless displays of virtuous brutality—a little thunder certainly wouldn't wake her from her dreams. I lit a cigarette and stared into this dark wet world around me. The rain kept coming down.

I turned on the car lights and could see pools of water in the high grass. A flood—God breaking his promise and drowning the world again. And who would be saved this time? Two by two into the ark. God condemned all single, divorced ladies to death. Holding their small babies in their arms, women pleaded to be saved, but the Lord could only use two of a species—you had to have a mate to have a chance for survival. The flood will get us this time. Sarah, still a child, is guilty by association of her parents' crimes. And I will sit in my watery grave at the foot of Ararat, cursing the facts of biology. Mammalian reproduction needs two, not one. A paramecium or an amoeba could climb aboard the ark even if its loved one had already been drowned in the first downfall.

At last dawn, gray with lighter rains, and I started the car up. The wet motor resisted, turned over, stalled, stopped and finally started. I drove slowly, afraid of skidding on the damp road, afraid of the strange landscape—flat stretches of empty country. My body was still cramped and my eyes ached. Sarah wanted breakfast, wanted to brush her teeth, and I searched the side of the road, eager for a place to stop.

For a long time Alex and I had pretended a normality we didn't feel. We were married, we had a child, we went to dinner parties, openings, lofts and galleries. We went to the park together on Sundays, following Sarah like two mummies come to life in an Egyptian horror movie. At night we would lie crumpled and limp on the bed, reading newspapers, mystery stories. I thought of turning our bedroom into a hothouse, of transporting dirt up the elevator and dumping it on our floor, and putting violet, fluorescent bulbs in the ceiling, and growing things about our bed—useful things like celery and carrots. But then at last Alex stirred. He put me face to the wall like a canvas that hadn't quite worked out and went on to other women. I heard them laughing together in living rooms and bars.

"I am a victim of life," I said wryly to friends, who looked at me uncomprehending. "You have to be a victim to understand a victim. Tied to the railroad tracks, hearing the whistle of the train rounding the bend, one understands all those flat on their backs waiting for the worst to happen." My friends looked away, averting their eyes from mine, so I stopped trying to tell them how the world looked from the ground up.

At last we got to the promised inn, which was an old farmhouse run by an old lady whose husband had been the local blacksmith half a century ago. She drank a jigger of Scotch each night, carefully measured in a little cup she kept on a special shelf in her immaculate kitchen that was covered with little sayings in sampler form. "God Bless Our Happy Home." "God Helps Those . . ." etc. She also had, hanging on the ice box door, a calendar from the local bank. It showed a picture of a volcano in Hawaii as its contribution to June. Our room had faded flowered wallpaper and a green quilt on the bed. I was so pleased not to be in a motel, to be someplace where a particular life had taken root and stubbornly survived. My fatigue lifted. Mrs. Swain fixed us a good breakfast and allowed Sarah to go into the front parlor to watch the color TV that rested on a little table covered with a large crocheted doily.

We spent all day and the following night in Brisketville, Oklahoma. When the rain stopped, I went for a walk in the fields, pushing away the crowds of June mosquitoes that swarmed about my bare legs. I sat down on the earth and admired its dark color. I looked at worms, wild flowers and my own dirty toes muddied from the wet ground. My courage came back. I need not be attached to anyone. By myself, I could forge across the country and, like my grandparents, I would learn to disconnect the past from the present, so the double albatross of loss and grief would fall from my neck when at last, like the ancient mariner, I had suffered enough.

After another hundred miles of driving we reached the reservation. Signs said "Cherokee Trading Post." We followed the arrows up a long winding dirt road and found an asphalt parking lot awaiting us at the top. The log-cabin trading post had a neon sign that advertised souvenirs, cigarettes and post cards in alternating green and blue lights. Sarah turned around in the back seat. "Look, mother, it's neat—it's really neat!" And so we entered the shop. An Indian woman looked at us without a flicker of greed—or even interest.

"Before we buy anything I want to see the reservation, meet the Indians. Don't you think, Sarah, the souvenirs will have more meaning later?" Sarah was pressing a hand against her left ear with a strained look on her face. "Anything the matter?" I asked.

"No, no, I'm fine." Sarah never admitted to vulnerability unless in dire extremity. I ignored the sense of anxiety I felt and requested the ten-dollar tour. The lady behind the counter took our money and directed us to the Indian Department Headquarters. We walked about half a mile to a cement bungalow where a representative from the Indian Affairs Office in Washington had his office. A young boy was offered us as a guide, and we set out in the jeep that seemed to belong to the wife of the Affairs officer. The back seat was filled with bags of dirty diapers that the young boy had agreed to deposit at the laundromat.

I looked up at the Oklahoma sky. Here we were, representatives of the destroying race, cultural barbarians ourselves, killing the buffalo, killing the long night of Indian memory. In the Bronx we once had a bonfire in an empty lot and the boys war-whooped around and I dreamed of being Pocahontas wrapping my brown arms around the threatened head of Captain John Smith. My reward, a trip to London, where in dresses and tight shoes, stared at by strangers, I would sink in loneliness and isolation till one night, whispering the loved name of my grandfather Chief Red Feather into the London fog, I would disappear, deaf to the chimes of Big Ben welcoming in the morning.

Sarah complained about the smell in the jeep, and I figured, by the large piles of diapers, that the wife of the local head of Indian Affairs had not been taught rudimentary birth control methods. We stopped at the school, which looked like a public school anywhere—cut-out gay Easter bunnies and tulips decorated the windows. Only the names on the children's cubbies told us that we were in Indian country, otherwise I would have been convinced I was in Long Island. "The children are learning the new math and have started using the Cuisenaire rods," my guide informed us. Sarah seemed restless in the empty school, banging her ear with her arm in a constant rhythm.

We drove. As we moved through the Oklahoma plains, our guide spoke of his plan to enter Texas Christian University the following year and of his hope to become an advertising man or do film work.

"Leave the reservation?"

"Of course," he said, "if I want to make something of myself."

We stopped in the middle of nowhere beneath a sky that seemed to stretch above us like a gauze bandage and filled up on gas in a station placed like a lone sentry out on the winding road. We drove past the church—Methodist—with small children playing on a rundown jungle gym and old tires. We drove past houses, small farmhouses with front porches, tar roofs and television antennas. We stopped and spoke with Mrs. Cloudsaway, who took us into her kitchen. Spotless red oilcloth covered the table and a portrait of Jackie Kennedy hung over the sink.

She welcomed me with her impassive Indian face, and complained to the guide that she could get no hot water in her pump. She was wearing a cotton print dress and slippers.

Sarah's face was flushed. "Aren't you a real Indian?" she said.

"Yes, yes," said Mrs. Cloudsaway, "but we only dress for special occasions. Here is my father's headdress," and she opened a closet door, pulling out a wealth of dyed feathers.

She spread the plumage on the faded corduroy couch for Sarah to examine. Sarah seemed mollified but not happy. Her eyes had a peculiar glaze over them. To the victor goes the culture, Sarah, you might just as well learn it now, I thought, aching nevertheless for the images of teepees and rain dances and bows and arrows slung over the naked shoulders of fine braves that must have caused her to anticipate this visit with pleasure.

Mrs. Cloudsaway's husband was working at Indian crafts at the Community Center, and we stopped by there. Men lounged against the walls of the Quonset hut and played mumbly peg or some form of knife game in the dry dirt. On tables inside, some men were making wooden flutes, painting masks and pasting feathers onto headbands. It looked like a kindergarten program in an old army barracks. Boxes of clearly labeled supplies stood at the back of the room, and a lady who introduced herself as a psychiatric social worker from Oklahoma City handed out crayons and glue. We stayed and watched awhile—the Running Deer, the Brave Elk, the fishermen spearing the weaving trout, all gone, transformed into little children playing where men once worked—internment camps are the same the world over.

The stupid ones, the souls rotting on the vine, the defenders of property, of virtue and old-fashioned exclusiveness—"I have and you don't"—the despisers of those who are different, at odds, colored or poor—they always are in power, making plans for the others; they have all the strength, standing like Uncle Sam, straight and tall, smiling into the future, while we, like the spirit of the

Siamese brother deprived of the necessary liver, hover about the lips, searching a way to get in past the clenched teeth, a way to become American ourselves. On the left, the idealists and dreamers are disembodied; against the anus or the nostrils or the ear, we push and are repelled again and again. Real life always vanquishes ghosts. The most we can hope for is to drive the righteous Mr. America crazy.

Our tour was almost over. We drove back across the reservation. Turning down a small dirt road, we came to a parking lot and a square cement building bearing the neon legend "Laundromat." We got out of the car, the young guide struggling with his bags of diapers. In the building were over fifty women waiting their turns at the ten machines that were churning and whirling with a sound of primitive pleasure or pain. Soap was dispensed in return for a coupon by a Mrs. Firebird. She took the diapers with a big broken-toothed smile. Sarah and I were introduced. The ladies stopped their casual chatter to stare at us. I felt uncomfortable. I did not want to be the focus of curiosity. I had come to do the staring myself. I felt angry—for my ten dollars for this tour, I shouldn't be made uncomfortable. I had to break the ice.

"Those are a lot of diapers," I said, "can I help you?" I reached into the nearest bag and pulled out a handful used by babies in obvious good health.

"Nice lady," said Mrs. Firebird. "Thank you."

I thought she might protest or stop me, but she must have felt it rude to cut off my gesture of friendship, and so I helped her load several machines.

Sarah looked at me as if I were a lunatic and went out on the porch to play jacks. "I'm hot," she said, and she looked flushed and dazed. Was she so disappointed that Indians were now just poor people with a special welfare system? I wondered.

I chatted about detergents with several of the women. Their preferences were the soaps advertised on TV the most frequently. Particularly they liked the White Tornado because it did the fastest job—"One cycle enough," said Mrs. Cornflower.

"How many children?" Mrs. Firebird asked.

"One—just the one outside," I said.

"Oh!" said the woman, looking at me sadly. "Poor lady."

I thought about explaining about the population explosion, but then I realized I was after all a producer of a small crop, and its worth was questionable.

"No man?" asked Mrs. Cornflower.

"No," I said.

"Oh," said the woman.

I could feel a lament for my singleness ride through the crowd; even the machines seemed quieted by the awesomeness of my plight. There were murmurs in the group. Someone offered me a Mars bar. I took it with my hands that now smelled unappetizingly of diapers. I took a bite and realized the lady next to me had reached out her hand. I passed it on—a peace pipe ceremony? I smiled at my new friends.

"Can you stay tonight?" Mrs. Firebird asked. "Because tonight we go to church, our true church—we have a special ceremony, maybe you know—we have the mushroom to bring us closer to God, and He will comfort you," she said, patting me steadily on my shoulders with her big hand. "Tonight you have good dreams, and we all be with you, and you be with God tomorrow."

I thought of all the Village parties, all the dark nights of strange bottles passed around in little rooms. I had never taken anything—my grandmother's vision of life: a bed to lie in, accept your suffering; a fear that the inside crust of my brain would crumble like graham cracker and never be put together again; a sense that the true purpose of life was to care about others, not to sink in selfish contemplation—I had felt that Emily Brimberg was not created to merge with Nirvana and should not push destiny to irregular places. But here in Oklahoma where my grandfather had never been, I considered, an orgy of revelation, a true meeting of my hallucinated self with the unknown, beyond the edge of terror—why should I not go there, and in what better company could I possibly find myself? Could I not emerge from this experience a sort of Super Brimberg—a Hassid who has seen the Messiah on the other side of the hill, coming, coming, stuck in the mud of human erosion? Could I not see it all for myself?

"Is there music?" I asked Mrs. Firebird. I wanted to go over the cliff with tom-toms beating an ancestral dirge.

Mrs. Firebird said between mouthfuls of sticky chocolate, "Yes, yes, everything."

What a beautiful day this was going to be, after all.

"Your daughter," said an old Indian lady, "can stay with the other children at the Community Center. They are showing a Disney movie tonight, a cartoon about black-and-white dogs—Dalmatians, I think."

Sarah would be delighted, and I would be part of the tribe. I felt the women warm around me.

"Perhaps," said Mrs. Cornflower, "you can get a baby tonight. It happens sometimes."

Was it an orgy I was invited to, or an immaculate conception? I shivered in the moist room, tripped on one of the baskets of clothes, was steadied by a young woman with long black braids.

"Your hair is beautiful," I told her.

"Thank you," she said, "I use Miss Clairol's Hair So New. You should try it."

Nothing could spoil my pleasure in the night to come. I left the laundromat to find my guide smoking a cigarette outside. It was late afternoon; the view was hazy and soft. I saw the plains stretched out like the day of creation, waiting for Eve to take her first step on the hard dry earth.

I suddenly saw Sarah sitting against the cement wall, hunched up, hugging her knees, her head down. I went over.

"What's the matter, darling?" I said, aware I had forgotten her.

"I'm cold, very cold," she said in a weak voice. "My ear hurts way down in my head. I need my sweater," she whimpered.

I felt her forehead. It was very hot. She was clearly sick. I got her into the jeep and wrapped my arms around her to keep her warm. Her sweaters were back in our car. The guide explained that the nearest doctor was thirty miles away in the town of Elk City and that the reservation office had aspirin, first aid equipment, but no antibiotics or other medical supplies.

"A witch doctor, Indian herbs?" I asked.

The guide stiffened. "Please don't make fun of us. We are rapidly moving into the twentieth century. If any Indian gets sick, we drive into Elk City to see Dr. Cass. If we are very sick we go to the hospital in Clinton. The government pays our Medicare bills, and we have a Blue

Cross plan as well. Can't you afford a doctor for the little girl?" he asked, suddenly considerate and mannerly.

"Yes, yes," I said, and drove away from the reservation.

My grandmother always knew a specialist for any ailment you had. My grandfather could name the best heart men in every hospital in the Bronx. At the end, when she shriveled and wrinkled like a dried cocoon sitting in her velvet chair, I would look at her and think, the cocoon will break, a new grandmother will emerge. At the very end, she said to me each day, "What does Dr. Goldstein say?—Should we have a consultation, you think?" And now I was missing my night of the mushroom, my Indian initiation, my chance to be something more than Emily Brimberg, because Sarah was burning with fever, and I had to take her to a doctor miles away from the ceremony I had planned to join.

We drove with the radio blaring country music. Sarah, wrapped in a blanket, seemed to sleep in the back seat. We pulled into the town of Elk City; oil tanks, oil riggings, lit the way. Like stationary fireflies, the network of wires and flame made the early evening darkness seem mystical, as if illuminated cobwebs hung from the clouds and laced the Oklahoma night, waiting for victims to come irrevocably close. Smoke poured from processing chimneys, and pipelines crisscrossed the ground; derricks and trucks parked off the main road. I stopped to ask directions to Dr. Cass and heard the heavy pumps like wounded dragons breathing in pain. We drove away from the oil fields into the center of town. There on a street called Standard, I found a white frame house with a little sign. Dr. Cass was having his supper but left his table to see Sarah in his office, which must once have been the parlor. "Ear infection," he said; a shot of penicillin, antibiotics, aspirin. He was gentle, and he asked her where she was from and told her to stay awhile in Elk City and visit the zoo, which had a unique collection of snakes. He gave her a lollipop, promised me twenty-four hours would restore her to her old self. I paid him on the way out. A good country doctor, a man to depend on.

If he'd asked me to marry him on the spot, I would have accepted, but as we left (Sarah already feeling better because she had been taken care of), I glanced in the dining room window. There a wife and three children were laughing together at some joke. Was he deceiving her with a floozy nurse in the operating room at Clinton, or was her laughter real?

I found a motel, and we turned on the television, Sarah and I both watching a movie in which Bette Davis plays a murdering nanny. I took a long time to fall asleep. Oil trucks traveled up and down the road outside our window all through the night, convoys of trucks migrating north; the sound of men's voices in a nearby bar kept me alert to possible invasion, and during the early hours of the morning, I thought of Mrs. Firebird and Mrs. Cornflower in heaven without me.

I THREW AWAY the maps I had brought from New York. I was now close enough to Mexico to get there by asking directions. We were going into Texas, on the last lap of the trip, and I decided to avoid the highways and travel from small town to town on the back roads. I wanted to drive slowly, to see the cows with their heads all in the same direction, their udders swollen pink, covered with June bugs and summer ticks. I wanted to see corrals, broncos rocking up and down in the hard Texas dust. I had planned for us to spend six days or so crossing the state, not long enough to learn the culture or understand the language, but long enough for visual memories, smell and touch that could mean learning for both Sarah and me.

Sarah felt better in the morning, but she still had a fever, so stayed in bed with the television on. I went across the street to a coffee shop and brought back hamburgers and malteds that we ate on the thin green rug that covered the floor.

"We didn't buy any Indian souvenirs," Sarah said to me accusingly.

"Well," I said, "you were sick. I wanted to get you to Doctor Cass. You can buy Mexican souvenirs, flowered piggy banks, silver jewelry, bright-colored lace dresses, when we cross the border."

"I'm not interested in Mexican souvenirs," she said, turning away from me in disgust.

The day seemed to last forever. I read magazines—all I could concentrate on—the local newspaper with its long column on lost or stolen motorcycles. The hours dragged. I bought a pack of cards and Sarah and I played gin rummy. The air conditioner in the room was set for freezing, so we stayed under the covers despite the heat we could see rising like steam clouds from the pavement out the window.

Alex's face blurred several times in my memory as I tried to think of him through the long night. I had loved him so completely I could not conceive that he existed without me. I thought of him drinking in his favorite bar, entertaining the local crowd with a description of two yaks copulating in the Central Park Zoo before the embarrassed gaze of parents whose own bedroom habits were more private. I thought of him in the bathroom, screaming for the toilet paper I always forgot to buy. I remembered him vomiting up a barrelful of nervous gulping; an attempt to swallow himself and avoid the reflection in the mirror. The results were disgusting all over the bathroom floor, but nevertheless, as Alex lay in bed heaving and writhing with the terrors of dawn as only a man whose alcoholic night is ending knows them, I felt a worship, a love for the warrior who had gone to battle and found the vision before him so ugly, so frightening that he had turned his horse and run, hallucinating angels following him on his path, telling him of dangers before, beside and in front.

I had not known anyone who drank a lot before Alex. My grandfather thought the goyim were slightly inebriated all the time and that explained their erratic behavior. When I first met Alex, I admired his consumption of alcohol—like lifting weights or running the mile in four minutes, I thought it was masculine, godlike, to throw down glasses of burning liquor and lurch about, rambling words, pink eyes, urgent tones. It seemed as if I had left my childhood across a river and stood on the other bank proud of my long swim. Alex would attack other painters when drunk. He would loudly criticize their work and occasionally punch them in the stomach. I was sad when once he told one runt of a painter with a large mustache and Adler elevated shoes that his style had not improved since his early days when he had smeared his feces on the slats of his crib. The mustached artist put his head down on the bar and cried in humiliation. Alex was in some ways like a storm trooper, and I, Jewish maiden, thrilled by his alien nature, could never get over the fact that I was under the sheets with the enemy. Sometimes he would go silent, morose, pale, and sit for hours in front of his blank canvas washing and rewashing his brushes in a turpentine solution. At night he would stare at me as if I were a griffin made of stone decorating his bed. I would play music, read, cook great casseroles and make fresh bread and wait for the long silence to end—eventually he would speak again—always we were at a point further distant from each other, till at last the divide was too vast.

Sarah and I started out the following morning, relieved to be out of the motel, to be moving again. The day was bright, and sun glistened on the asphalt like the gold coin the prospectors had come to claim. Sarah played jacks, elevator, pigs in the pen, cherries in the basket. She was cheerful too. "I can't wait to see a real ranch," she said, "where they have a million steer, and cowboys ride horses, singing songs while they cook their bacon over a campfire." We crossed the border into Texas, and immediately the ground became dusty and there seemed to be fewer cars on the road. I took the first exit off the highway, and we drove past small farms, a shopping center that advertised its goods in such big letters you knew the price of three boxes of frozen carrots a mile away. We passed a long automobile graveyard where the cars were piled high like bones in burial mounds, and the twisted chrome and metal reflected the sunlight back into the white sky. An end to getaway cars, family picnic cars, cars that drove men out to the oil fields, sister to the movies on Saturday night—memories spun about the dead heap like so many worms crawling among the corpses. We followed the signs south, avoiding Amarillo, which promised to be too big a town. Sarah seemed happy that the long trip was nearly over. She asked me at least three times on what day her school started in September, as if repetition would bring it closer. The sun began to soften toward the afternoon, and I started to look for a place to stay. I asked at a gas station where an unfriendly attendant with a shotgun in his hand waved me silently on.

I saw signs that said "Settlement Tomorrow," and arrows pointing south. I decided that we would try Settlement Tomorrow and see if it was a ranch, a commune (a group of professors from Stanford and Berkeley planning an ideal future for the human race, a group of religious fanatics who never had sex, but had found the secret of immortality, a home for unwed mothers complete with psychiatric counseling). A gnawing curiosity made me speed up the car, take turns with an unusual confidence. I passed the scrubby trees, the cactus and wide ferns, the gray dirt and the large boulders, without even appreciating that we were being drawn into a hot desert that was empty of other human life. I saw more signs pointing to "Settlement Tomorrow," and I felt closer to my destination. Was I headed toward a home for the mentally retarded learning simple vocational skills, or would it be a hip family of youngsters whose parents never understood and never would?

At last, as I was turning the possibilities over in my mind, I saw it up ahead: a gathering, a herd, of trailers with a large sign in front saying, "Welcome–Settlement Tomorrow." I was sure that whatever the place, Sarah and I could spend the night and continue south the following day. I pulled the car up in front of the first trailer. I noticed its wheels were gone and a little orange-and-white plastic awning covered the back door. A clothesline was attached to a pole, and a few large flowery dresses floated in the slight breeze. Several green plants grew in orange juice cans placed about what could be considered a yard.

"Here, Mother? You want to stop *here?* They probably don't have any running water. How can I take my medicine? How can I brush my teeth?"

"Here, Sarah, it has to be," I said, realizing I was too tired to go on, no matter what. It was clearly not an architectural school. That was one possibility eliminated. The face of a very old lady suddenly appeared, looking at us from between the venetian blinds on the trailer window. I smiled, trying to look friendly.

The old lady hobbled down the little steps and came over. Her fine hair was rinsed bright blue, and she had Ace bandages on her wrists and ankles. She was wrinkled and her flesh sagged and folded strangely, but her smile was warm and welcoming. Sarah backed off, leaving me to extend my hand and my name.

"Mrs. Johnson," I said. "My daughter and I are seeing the country and have found ourselves on your doorstep."

"Welcome, welcome, so happy to have you," the little lady crooned. "You must spend the night, as long as you like, it's too far to leave us now. You'll have supper with me, and your pretty daughter's name?"

Sarah reluctantly gave her the information.

"How old are you, darling?"

"Ten," Sarah said, not looking up.

"So tall you are, Ha! You want to see my china doll collection?"

Sarah looked up, managed an agreeable smile.

"Do let's get out of this heat," the old lady said, but, as we moved toward her trailer, I heard the flickering of a dozen blinds and the opening and closing of doors, and suddenly we were surrounded by a crowd of old men and women, looking, pointing, talking about us.

A very ancient person of uncertain sex hobbled up to us on crutches. "Ida Newsoms," she said; "Lost my leg just last Friday and here I am walking around as well as ever. Welcome to our little colony—my husband and I, bless his soul, come here out of Houston seventeen years ago, and I bet our trailer has grown roots right down to the bottom of the desert." She cackled.

"Mrs. Johnson," I introduced myself. "Sarah and I are seeing the country."

"What a dear little girl. I made some chocolate fudge this afternoon. A good fairy must have told me you were stopping by."

Sarah seemed less frightened than I was by the apparition of death that showed in Mrs. Newsoms' veins and her puffy skin. Sarah looked up at the word fudge, and she smiled warmly at the one-legged lady.

"Let's go over to Community and have a little refreshment."

"Community" turned out to be about eight trailers parked end to end, gifts of members of this senior citizens' society who had died, creating a central meeting place for their remaining friends. A Victrola played Guy Lombardo songs. A bookcase held games: chess, checkers, Chinese Checkers, Monopoly, Go Fish and Old Maid. Card tables were placed in the center of one trailer; a bulletin board listed the day's activities: bowling, canasta, Mah-Jongg, cooking classes, flower-arranging classes, newspaper editorial board meetings, counsel meetings, painting. Doctor's visit at 3:00—a list of those who signed for appointments went on for three pages. Square dancing at 8:00 and a folk sing at 9:00. The folks at Settlement Tomorrow had organized their lives so that each member would be a part of a whole, busy within the group.

"Looking forward to a happy tomorrow," explained Mr. James Reid, who introduced himself. The oldest man around, his leadership qualities were unaffected by the fact that his voice had only the volume of a soft whisper. He told me he had come to Texas after forty years of running a shirt business, a little factory in Toledo. He had retired, "a mistake for a man of my energy," he reported; his sons-in-law ran the business, not at all well, he confided, and like a dispossessed Lear, he had wandered from Miami to St. Petersburg without root or purpose. At last someone suggested Settlement Tomorrow, and here he had found friends—he put his arms around two plump old ladies who giggled and blushed—and had lived happily for eight years and intended to live, he whispered solemnly, "at least until tomorrow. . . ."

Sarah was served fudge and milk by Mrs. Newsoms and then joined a group of ladies at a card table. They were cutting out paper dolls to use as decoration for a bulletin board. I heard Sarah laughing as the women at the table turned warm and admiring eyes toward her: "Cheeks are so round"—"She cuts so well"—"Such skill with scissors"—"Her hair is so shiny"—"What a pretty smile!"

I had a cup of tea made with mineral water and chatted with several of the old people. Soon I told them I was getting a divorce. So sad, they said. Such a pretty young thing. He must have been a brute, not to appreciate you. Why should they assume he rejected me? Was it in my posture, or is the woman always the discard? I felt uncomfortable that strangers should come so close. But these were not ordinary strangers. They were so warm and giving. They seemed to presume a long acquaintance with me, even a kind of relationship or kinship that made any personal intrusion possible.

"I've been divorced now forty-five years, and let me tell you there hasn't been a day gone by, I'm not grateful that I left that smelly Eugene. He picked his nose at the dinner table." A skinny lady with roses painted on her sunken cheeks patted me on the shoulder.

A sisterhood was instantly formed. "Did you ever remarry?" I asked.

"What for?" she said. "Eugene paid me well enough; no man is best of all. I got here, and now we are like married people all living for each other—only it's nice—I mean now I'm never going to die till I have to."

"Have some fudge." Ida offered me some delicious warm chocolate fudge.

The music switched to "Mairsy doats and dozey doats and liddell lambsy divey," sung by Frank Sinatra, whose voice still carried sex appeal across the years.

Sarah was holding a porcelain doll one of the women had brought her . . . "used to be my daughter's, left it when she went to nursing school in St. Louis, and she never came back for it—been just laying here waiting for some little girl like you to come along and love . . ." I hadn't seen Sarah play with dolls for several years, and then only to act out with friends some familiar television comedy, but now her eyes were shining, and she hugged the new acquisition close to her. Had I ignored my daughter? was more going on than I had thought? did my own vague preoccupations, the blankness of my nights, reading mystery stories till Alex returned from his private prowls, was my vision of my child blunted? Sarah, I thought, I could have bought you a porcelain doll if I'd known you wanted one—but would Sarah have wanted a doll from me, or was it the old lady's hand stroking her hair, the wrinkled fingers holding the small smooth head, that made the doll so precious?

"Let's have a tea party," said a monstrous old lady, whose fat legs shuffled about in cut-open bedroom slippers. The access to the vagina seemed impossible. Instantly a lace cloth covered one of the bridge tables, and cookies were placed on the table. Tea cups and dolls pulled out of sewing baskets, from under chairs and behind the flowered curtains that covered the small trailer windows. "Often we have tea parties for ourselves and our favorite dolls," the moonfaced lady said. I felt uncomfortable as the dolls were put in position, and the tea was heated and served—embarrassed for the childishness of the aged—the sweetness of little girls in old women seemed so sad, edged in memories that could not be erased. This doll's tea party was not practice for the real thing, but a pretense that the real thing had never happened; and it had a rawness to it that made me look out the window at the expanse of desert, the water tanks that kept the community, the electric generator with its continuous curling wires like a great toad, at the sand surrounded by scrub cactus and a gray rock or two.

I heard Sarah laugh out loud. She was enjoying the party. One of the women was showing her how her teeth could come in and out. She placed her bridge on the table, her face strange, like the empty geranium pot my grandmother kept in the kitchen to store string and cord from packages in case they might one day be needed. Sarah thought the removable teeth one of the miracles of the world.

I moved away from the party and tried to join some men playing poker in the next trailer. "Man's game, man's game, no ladies; sorry, miss, no ladies allowed," one old codger leered at me while pushing me back with his non-card-holding hand.

I walked on past a cabinet filled with trading cards that had pictures of well-known football and baseball players printed on them. I really would have liked to have left Settlement Tomorrow at once, but I knew it would soon be dark. I didn't know where to go or how to get anywhere. The desert was not safe for a woman used to the streets of the Bronx. And Sarah seemed so happy that I felt I couldn't wrench her from the party and take her into another lonely night with me and the car.

I walked on to a third trailer where there was a bingo game going on. Both sexes were participating.

"Come on, honey, you play," said a friendly voice. A nice old man with a sweet smile looked up at me.

What else? Why not? I took a card from the box in the center of the table and sat down. I smiled at the ring of faces that stared at me, warm and bubbling.

"What pretty hair"—"What blue eyes"—"Such an intelligent face"—"Good taste in clothes. . . ." A murmur of approval went about the tables. They talked about me almost as if I weren't there . . . as if they towered above me and in my smallness I would not hear or observe their looks and words. I felt a little silly but pleased. They liked me after all, and I felt a circle tighten around me, surround me. I was not an alien, a loner; I was somehow part of them, at least, of their game. The caller shouted out the numbers, and I became involved in completing my lines. Someone brought us coffee. The winners won little prizes in boxes—a comb, a lipstick, a pair of stretch socks, a plastic flower. I wanted to win something. I had been a loser long enough.

An alarm clock sounded. They started to put the game away. I felt disappointed.

"Here," said a lady, "a prize for you for being new. This is your first night—everyone gets a prize on their first night."

I started to protest, but everyone laughed so good-naturedly, I opened it and thanked them all for the handsome bottle of perfume I had not legitimately won. It was the dinner hour and the community trailers emptied.

Sarah and I went back with Ida Newsoms to her trailer, and she cooked us lamb chops and vegetables. We ate on plastic trays on her steps, watching the sun go down over the desert, listening to the sounds of running water, the voices in the other trailers. Sarah kept her porcelain doll on her lap; she whispered to the doll occasionally. She seemed younger out here in the middle of nowhere, surrounded by people at the edge of the grave—people whose trailers had been purchased for trips around the country to see what they had missed and then, after a little adventure, they had bunched together, like horseshoe crabs in the mating season, to find a Golden Age. They were laid out on the desert, baking till they disintegrate, return to the hard earth, leaving behind the trailer cocoon filled with plastic items—toothbrushes, glasses, place mats—all the non-biodegradable mucus of an otherwise unmarked existence.

I walked a little way out of the settlement. Night in the desert is different than anywhere else, quiet, the distance to the nearest group of large rocks seemed a thousand miles. The moon reflected on the sand, a flat dead light. I felt like the ancient mariner whose boat was marooned in a rank and dreadful place. Behind me I saw the TV antennas rising from the trailer roofs like broken ladders to the sky—Joseph sold into Egypt must have looked out the wagon curtains and seen the desert sand moving beneath the wagon wheels, carrying him away from his beloved father, from home, into the empty unknown. How frightened he must have been! And his mother, weeping in her tent, must have felt as if part of her body had been broken off and all her blood was draining away into the sand as she grieved for the son she had thought was hers forever.

Suddenly I had to urinate—a steady pressure had built up in my bladder. I realized that hours had gone by, and that I had known I should use a bathroom, but the faint smell of a leaking cesspool around the settlement had made me suspect the bathroom of other horrors, and so I had ignored the steady signals. Now I really could wait no longer. I thought of running back to the trailers, but felt I could not make it. Certainly I could not make it with anything resembling dignity, so I took off my slacks, took off my underpants, and in the light of the full moon squatted down on the desert; like a lizard or a gopher or horny toad, I let my urine run into the sand. At last it is absorbed with just a dark trace of momentary dampness on the ground surface. Men are so pleased with their long stream, their fountainhead jutting urine, directing it where they will. But I am awed by the dark pool of water that gathers mysterious on the ground between my legs; a Grendel swims in a little lake, life began in a body of water. To make a pond with a shifting muddy bottom, with a story of its own—that too is a thing of beauty.

It was cool on the desert and I felt wet and ashamed, ashamed of my waste products, of my naked vagina drying in the chilled night air. No one was looking at me, and yet I felt, listening to a distant animal howl at his mate, I am guilty of transgression; perhaps one simply should not be alone—aloneness itself is shameful. I dressed and hurried back to the trailers.

Sarah was sitting on the fat lady's lumpy large lap, her head on her shoulder, her long legs dangling down, watching a TV program. I sat down next to a man whose bright blue eyes were concentrated on the old magazines he was going through; occasionally he would cut something out of a magazine and paste it in a notebook that rested on his knees. He noticed me watching him. He smiled sweetly, "Come see what I'm doing. I'm making a scrapbook," he said, "of all the things I always wanted to have and didn't get. It's going to be a record of memories of things I didn't have. Look here," and he opened it. I saw a long-finned Cadillac, a freezer icebox, a trip to Hawaii advertised in a picture of blue palms illuminated by the glowing lights of a modern hotel. I saw a picture of a baby girl in a little pink bonnet. I asked him about it. "Oh, we only had sons . . . three of them. I always wanted a daughter—here she is." He pointed to the page. "I've named her Annette after my wife." He insisted I look on and on at the many pages filled with sterling silver, Waring Blenders, theater advertisements of shows he missed because the touring company never came to Amarillo, suede shoes, garden shears—his missed memories were many.

He seemed so blithe and happy that I could only suppose all his disappointments stayed inside the scrapbook, leaving his soul in untormented peace. I finally disengaged Sarah from the lap she was sitting on and put her to bed in a little bunk in Mrs. Newsoms' trailer. Mrs. Newsoms tucked her in, telling her a story about three princesses who all wanted to marry the same prince. Too tame, I thought, for a girl who watched "Mod Squad" every Tuesday night, but Sarah listened intently while I tested my wordpower in an old *Reader's Digest* that was kept on the shelf above the bed. The bathrooms were set up in one of the legacy trailers and really the odor was strong in the vicinity of one hundred feet around. I asked Mrs. Newsoms about it.

"Oh, dear," she said, "we get so used to little inconveniences out here. The cesspool has developed a crack, and it just takes the plumber forever to get himself out here. We just fuss over him all the time when he comes. We made him cookies and lemonade last time, and Martha knit him a pair of argyle socks, but it's still taken him forever to answer our call. There's a telephone in the Community trailer—I'll call him again tomorrow. Some of the fellows are going into town for groceries in the next day or two, I'll remind them to go talk to him."

With that she wished me sweet dreams, pulled out a bed that was tucked under a seat, and left with the television on, the *Reader's Digest* to keep me company, while she went out to a meeting of all the members of Settlement Tomorrow.

"A sort of Town Hall," she said. I asked to go with her, but, no, she said, these meetings were just for members, and some of the old folks were suspicious of strangers. Old folks being the way they are. She patted me on the shoulder and said good-night. I felt somehow disgruntled, abandoned. After all, she had every right to go out and leave me—I was just a stranger who had dropped in that afternoon. But she had put on earrings and powdered her face, and I had the odd feeling someone was having a party and I was left out, not even allowed in to pass the hors d'oeuvres. I watched a movie, the eleven o'clock news and fell asleep.

I dreamed I removed my diaphragm, but it was filled with holes like a salad sieve. A little boy came and took it from my hands, putting it on his head like a yarmulka.

I wanted it—why should little boys get to wear yarmulkas and girls be without any special distinction? I slept fitfully—the strange narrow place—the bed was hard. At one point I opened my eyes, and I saw the room filled with the old people peering down at me, whispering to each other. I sat up, cold with fear.

But they all smiled and nodded, "Just came to see that you didn't need anything"—"to make sure you're comfortable."

Ida brought me a drink of water and put it by the bedside. I lay back reassured and closed my eyes. I felt the old people in the trailer; by my bed, I heard chucklings and cooings.

"Isn't she sweet sleeping, I could just kiss her."

Someone straightened my blanket. I felt a dry hand on my forehead. I wanted them to go away, but I sensed the warmth that was coming from them, and I did not want to be rude, so I lay there feigning sleep while they stood about.

"Those clothes are good, New York clothes," one said.

"Well, she'll get used to it; I can do some nice things for her on the sewing machine."

I heard mumblings of one kind or another, and at last I sensed the trailer was empty. I sat up and looked out the venetian blind on the little window by the bed. I looked straight into the face of an old man who was staring in. He must have been standing on a box or something, trying to get a look. After I recovered from my initial startle, I had to smile—such an old Peeping Tom! Well, more credit to him—hope he saw something he liked. I finally fell back asleep.

When I woke in the morning, the smell of good coffee filled the trailer. Sarah was toasting English muffins and told me she was going to start making furniture for a doll's house. I explained that we would be leaving after breakfast, and there was no time for lengthy projects.

"Oh, I think there is," said Mrs. Newsoms with a sweet and mysterious smile.

"Thank you for your hospitality. I appreciate it so much, but I must go to Juarez for my divorce. I must be there in just a few days."

"Formalities, my dear, don't worry about formalities. He's not with you, that's a real good divorce. Papers won't make it any better."

Reason was on her side, but I still wanted to get to Juarez, my destination, my symbolic point of departure into a single existence. It would be nice, I thought, if men could be legally punished for insufficient loving, for caring too much about their ambitions, for lack of tenderness, or concern, for sexual fickleness, for animal behavior, for seeking vaginas that didn't claim attention in the mornings. Tried and convicted, imprisoned; they should be placed naked in a hole, unable to stand or sit, they should bend their spines in abject humiliation. They should be fed regrets with nails floating in their porridge. They should be tarred and feathered at least once a week, and daily their penises should be stimulated till enlarged, then dipped in glue and covered with shellac till they looked like pieces of furniture discarded in a corner of a Salvation Army thrift shop.

"Stay for lunch at least," said Ida Newsoms. "You should walk around a little and get to know our little section of Texas."

"No," I said firmly, "Juarez is where I'm going. Sarah, have you packed your nightgown?"

"I'd like to stay," she said. "I really like it here a lot. I mean I'm tired of driving all the time."

Her voice was whiney, her lips sullen. She glared at me—mother-interferer!—I felt the hate and the anger move across the room at me like a fog across the moors. Was it about power, who told whom what to do when? Was it about her father, who possibly loved her when he could find the time? Was it just natural that she should despise me, or was it my failure, another failure? She kicked at the trailer wall with her foot.

"You're a stupid," she said, bursting into tears and jumping out of the trailer. On all this good earth there may be no bigger stupid, I felt, but what could I do? I sadly ate my English muffin and drank the good coffee Mrs. Newsoms insisted I have.

"What did your husband do?" I asked to make conversation, to shake myself away from the dark apparition of Sarah's disgruntled soul.

"Well, dear," she said, "Hubert ran off and left me some twenty years ago. He said one night as we were getting into bed, 'I'm tired of paying bills—I'm sick of your going to the hairdresser on Wednesday and of buying you new shoes each Easter, and I'm sick of fixing the windows every time a screen breaks, and I'm sick of paying grocery bills when I only eat half the food, and I'm sick of buying you new gold for your teeth, and I'm sick of paying for the corsets and bras and all that other junk you put on yourself. I'm moving out where my work will pay for me, like a self-respecting person should. You go out and get yourself a job and pay for yourself or starve.' The next morning he left, packed everything—the bowling trophy, his mother's hot plate, everything—and left. I tried to chase him down, to get the courts to force him to give me alimony, but he had done a jack-rabbit trick of going down a hole none of us was skinny or mean enough to follow. So there I was in Almaden, Arkansas, poor as a churchmouse, fifty years old—fat as a house, educated like a nigger—what could I do?

"I tell you what I did. I cried a lot, a week or two—my sister sent food to the house—and then I thought, why not just show that son-of-a-bitch mean bastard who never mentioned minding paying for me when he was trying to get into my pants? I turned my house into a house of God, and I appointed myself preacher-lady. I let it get around I had some good cures. Folks took it from there, and some said I could see the future. And I took a part of the plate at every meeting we had, and I told fortunes and futures and dispensed a little homemade medicine, and I made out just fine. After the first two months, I realized that Hubert with his measly little supervisory job at the mill had been keeping a good woman down and out. I saved. I traveled in the deer-hunting season when a lot of my business fell off. I been to Paris and Rome on excursion trips. I bought a trailer for my old age. I done all right without that Hubert." She laughed and laughed, though I felt the joke was not on Hubert.

"Tell me my fortune," I said impulsively.

"Not for free," she said. "I'm a professional—two dollars."

"All right." I gave her the money, though I was disappointed because I had thought we were friends.

She looked at my palms, she felt around my head, she took my pulse while staring me in the eye. At last she said, "You are going to be in Texas a long while—you are going to change your plans. You have traveled long and far enough—now it is time to rest among friends. They will care for you, protect you from loneliness, godlessness, marauders in the night. I see a long future in a dry place, health and wealth will be yours. You are going to be surprised at what happens to you." With that she slapped her thigh and laughed so warmly I laughed too.

"I guess," I said, "the future is always a surprise."

"Sometimes," she laughed some more, "it's not so much of a surprise as you would think."

I refused another drink of coffee, feeling that I had to wrench myself away. A kind of exhaustion was beginning to overwhelm me, although it was so early in the morning—probably the fatigue of so many days' driving, of time lasting so long and hanging so shapeless around me. I thought for a second of taking another day in Settlement Tomorrow, of playing cards in the afternoon and reading magazines in the community trailers . . . but I remembered Manuelo Desprito was expecting me. This was not a suitable place to stop my life from running where it would. I excused myself.

I put our little suitcases in the car. I found Sarah in the Community trailer playing gin rummy with an old man who could hear almost nothing, so she had to shout goodbye when I insisted she leave. She kissed several of the ladies goodbye and without looking at me, allowing a distance as deep as the Grand Canyon between us, she climbed into the back of the wagon. A large crowd had gathered around to wave us off, or so I thought. I smiled cheerfully, thanked everyone, put the key in the ignition, turned it, stepped on the motor. Nothing happened. I tried again. I had put gas in it the day before, water and oil. I tried again. I waited a minute or two—the crowd outside came closer to the car. Some stood directly in front. I tried to wave them off, but they didn't move. I attempted the ignition again. The car made no sound. Like a corpse it rested on its wheels, unresponsive, immobile. I wanted to scream in rage, to tear its chrome fenders off with my bare hands, to beg it, to plead with it to start.

I got out. Won't somebody help—who knows about cars? I smiled endearingly at the men. Once they were boys covered with grease, riding about the roads in cars that they had put together themselves. But no one stepped forward. They just shook their heads at me, looked up at the clear morning sky. I decided to open the hood; maybe if I exposed the motor someone would come to my aid. I struggled to find the catch that springs the hood. It was very hot and I was perspiring badly. Aware of the wet circles around my underarms, I became embarrassed. At last the hood jumped up, and I saw the mass of wires and battery box and spark plugs; dark and greasy, the motor lay revealed. I stared for a few moments, and then I saw wires cut, hanging at peculiar angles. I looked down at my tires and saw the air had been released.

But why? Who—I turned to the silent crowd—what could this mean? No angry blacks, no drug addicts, no juvenile delinquents in Settlement Tomorrow—why had my car been attacked? What was I going to do? I felt small, even afraid of the stern faces looking steadily at me. What had I ever done to them? Who did it? "Who did this?" I screamed.

Silence.

"What does it mean? Tell me please," I begged Ida Newsoms.

"Now don't get yourself so excited," she said. "The young are so impatient—sometimes you have to change your plans—sometimes you just have to do things that other people expect you to do—you can't just be thinking of yourself all the time. That's not really nice, is it?"

I felt obscurely guilty. I didn't quite see why, but I knew that in some way I had been selfish—but what was she talking about? I lit a cigarette to cover my growing panic. The crowd moved closer, leaning against my useless car. One of the men, wheezing and coughing, pulled my suitcases out of the back seat. I wanted to stop him, but what for? The car would not, I now knew, be starting.

"I really must be on my way," I smiled sweetly at them all. "May I use the phone? I'll call the garage or the sheriff."

"No," said Ida. "I don't think you should do that."

The entire gang blocked my way to the central trailer where, I knew, the phone waited on a card table beneath a travel poster picturing the Alps covered with snow.

I looked at the somber faces of the old people staring at me. I sensed that peculiar kind of group solidarity among them that gave them a super-strength. I was not able to run through the group, so I tried cajoling.

"Now come on, be nice. I just want to walk past you, to phone to get my car fixed. I'm not going to bother anyone at Settlement Tomorrow. I'll send you a postcard from Mexico to put up on the bulletin board." I shouted so the deaf ones could understand me . . . they seemed to press closer about me like an undulating octopus feeling its way along the ocean floor.

"What do you want?" I asked. Money—of course, it was money. "Listen," I said, "I have one thousand dollars' worth of traveler's checks in my bag. I'll get it for you. I'll gladly sign it over to you as soon as you've given me the phone—or some one of you nice men," I smiled nervously, "fixes my car."

I saw the crowd coming closer. Some of the men were poking around in the motor with their canes; wires were flying about. A few of the old ladies, a little senile, I thought, had broken off from the main group and were singing "Camptown races back in town, oh do da day . . . Bet my money on the bobtailed nag, Somebody bet on the bay, do da, do, da, do." I looked at the faces near me—a certain desperation in the eyes, a fierce set to the mouths. I ran into the car, locked the doors and rolled up the windows.

Sarah said, "Mother, what's the matter with you? You act frightened of our friends—I'm sure they just want to help."

"Sarah, shut up!" I yelled at her. "You don't know what's going on at all—you're just a kid, and you're stupid and ignorant, besides," I shouted at the top of my lungs in a terrible rage. If she had been closer, I might have hit her, scratched at her eyes—a great frustration making me feel as if I was going to turn to antimatter in a moment, turn inside out like a glove, and let all my organs slither about on the car seat looking for the case, the frame, that had formerly enclosed them.

The very second I yelled at her, I wept with guilt: my poor baby, no family, no brothers or sisters, no big dog or horse or home in the country—just a screwed-to-the-breaking-point mother, and a father removed. Poor baby, who had not chosen to come to Texas in a car with a wilting woman who seemed to have gotten in some terrible trouble with some old people who were complete strangers yesterday, and now seemed part of a cast of millions in a possible tragedy in which Sarah was a participant.—My God, why had I yelled at her, when outside the window, now sitting on the fenders of the car, was an ancient mob of harridans and old warlocks who wanted something or other from me? . . .

I rolled the window down a little. "Do you want money?—Do you want cash?—The girl's father is rich, he could wire it to you if you wanted."

This was bravado—I wasn't sure Alex would wire money to redeem Sarah or me. He had made a settlement, but despite being a rich man, on his own and through inheritance, I knew he resented every penny the lawyers had shamed him into giving me. If I could make my own way, have him eat his money, I would—a lifetime of monthly checks from him would drive me mad with humiliation. I planned to work as a doctor's receptionist, to sell hosiery in a department store—anything but take his severance pay forever. "How much money do you want?" I rolled the window down a little further. Ida pressed her face up close, no longer so friendly.

"Let me explain," said Ida. "You see, most all of us had children, and now we have grandchildren, and a few of us even have great-grandchildren." There were a few yay-hurrahs from the crowd. "We did our best for our children, school, clothes, Girl Scout groups, cameras, swimming lessons, orthodontists, dancing classes—we did what we could, not being rich or anything, we shared what we had, and we worried and we loved and planned so many things—most of those plans just never quite happened." A sigh of agreement went through the group. "Now many of us are without husbands or wives. We are sick often, and the money for things is almost gone, and each of us knows that our children hope we'll never call. They hope we'll never come to visit. They don't want to remember that death is the end of it all, that they were once newborn, suckling and helpless. Our grandchildren don't come to visit, they have other things to do—excuses are made, mentions of nice nursing homes in Phoenix or La Jolla. We are cut off by our children like a withered branch of a tree from the green and growing trunk. So we bake in the desert sun, our fingers itching to touch the smooth skin and fine hair, the sweet round bottoms of our grandchildren, and the memories of our children before they didn't like the way we cooked, the clothes we wore, before they hated us because we drank too much, or lost our job, or voted the wrong way in the last election.

"We are happy here in Settlement Tomorrow, but most of our children stop writing after a while. They don't send pictures any more—they forget. They have forgotten us."

I heard a cry in the crowd, the sound of tears on old skin. "But," I said, "I haven't forgotten anyone. I haven't done anything wrong."

"Of course not, of course not," Ida soothed me.

I felt more composed, but they were still pressing all around the car. Although they were old and weak, there were too many of them just to push aside. I noticed many were holding pots and frying pans, one an iron, another a crutch, in case I should try force.

"What do you want from me?" I cried out to all of them.

The heat was so strong I felt suffocated, as if there was cotton in my mouth, in my nostrils, in my chest. The smell of the cesspool rose in the hot air, and I felt nauseous and my legs trembled.

"My daughter," called out one old crone, "went to New York to become an actress. She once sent me a red wig from Saks Fifth Avenue, but I haven't heard from her for fifteen years."

Another spoke: "My son died of leukemia, my daughter-in-law took the children back east to her parents. I haven't heard from them since."

"But what's that got to do with me, my car?" I begged for an explanation. I turned from silent face to silent face—each staring at me peculiarly, lovingly.

Ida told me, "You're it—you and your daughter are going to be Settlement Tomorrow's daughter and granddaughter. We'll all share you very nicely—no one will hog you or anything like that. We'll love you and take care of you and play games with the child, and I think you'll be very happy. Let's get into the shade and have some iced tea."

By now the old people were all over the car. They were pressed against the back of the wagon. Some old man was playing puppets with his fingers, trying to make Sarah laugh, but Sarah had grasped that this was more than a game. "Mother, I'm frightened," she whined.

"It's all right," I said calmly, my own fear and panic shrinking in a hard knot at the center of my stomach as soon as I realized Sarah needed me. Obviously we were at least momentarily trapped—I couldn't force my way to the telephone, the car was a disaster. "Sarah," I said, "listen to me. These old people really seem to want us to stay with them, and I think we will for a while till I can figure a way out of here. Meantime you enjoy yourself with them, just don't argue with me if I give you an order to move fast some time or other."

I knew I sounded to her as if I had a plan—as if everything was in control. In fact I could barely think at all, so confused was I by the terrible menace of this group that had as its motive simply a desire to love me. I felt guilty, ungrateful, and yet I knew that I must not give up for a second, must grab the first opportunity to escape. I saw Mr. James Reid, his face pressed against the side window, looking at me. He was grinning—there was a lascivious, unfatherly look in his eyes as they surveyed my breasts. Of course he was fooling himself, remembering rather than experiencing, but still I felt uneasy. What might they expect of a community youth symbol?

"Okay," I shouted, "get away from the car, I'm coming out. Sarah and I will be happy to stay for a while." I managed a weak smile, a thin deceitful straggling smile, meant to deflect hostility.

"Hooray, Hooray, three cheers, Sis-boom Bah." I heard a football yell. I stood in the heat with the dust of the road moving like low fog on a wet New England night.

"I'm very thirsty," I said to Ida. My own voice sounded strange in my ears, curiously young and weak and high-pitched.

Sarah stood next to me, clutching the porcelain doll she'd been given the way she'd once held on to a pink blanket when I left her in the dark each night. I felt a hard pinch on my bottom. I wheeled around. There was Mr. James Reid, grinning innocently, his chin nearly resting on my shoulder.

A half hour later, Sarah was watching TV with several grandpas, and I was helping Ida shell peas on the back steps of her trailer. "We'll take real good care of you," she said. "No one will miss you, and you'll have the satisfaction of knowing you're leading a good Christian life."

I saw a ray of hope—a door in the walls that imprisoned me. "I'm Jewish," I said. "I've always been Jewish. I'm sure you don't want a Jewish daughter or granddaughter, so perhaps we should call a garage, so I could leave."

"You're Jewish, what do you know! I would never have guessed it. Of course I only met two Jewish people in my life, but there were a lot of Jews in Oklahoma City, my daddy said. They owned all the stores, got the money so tight no one else could get a hold of any. You're Jewish, just like Jesus—and you've come here to us—what a wonderful coincidence, isn't that nice? Do you eat anything special?" she asked solicitously, and I realized that intolerance—bigotry—only worked against Jews, never for them. I looked into her old face, smiling proudly at me as if I'd brought home a good report card. "What would you do differently if you could live again?" I asked.

"Everything," she said, "everything, and I guess I'd still be waiting for something wonderful to happen to me to change whichever choice I made. It all comes down to nothing but wishing, anyhow."

I thought maybe she was right but I still wanted to get out. I didn't look forward to days of bingo, years of dust and sand and cactus, of being stuck with the old folks, rotting among the near-dead, the already stinking. I still had hopes—if not for love, then at least for freedom, autonomy—expectations of a new tomorrow. I had to find a way out.

Suppose I failed—suppose I became a Jewish slave to the aged unloved. It seems unthinkable, but quite possible—Jews have been slaves before and would be again. I suddenly burst into tears, sobbing as I had never before, because the desert looked so wide and deep, and the distance to the next town too long to walk, too far to flee. I was truly a prisoner. My face got blotchy, my eyes swollen, and I cried on till at last I let myself be led inside the trailer, tucked into bed, the shades pulled down, the fan turned on. A little later, Ida tiptoed in and brought a pile of movie magazines and left them on the floor by the bed.

We could have stayed in a motel in Amarillo—there was no need to follow the signs to Settlement Tomorrow. I cursed my lack of judgment, my stupid curiosity. I looked out the window. No car came down the road. I had not heard or seen a car since my arrival, an age ago. I determined to plan an escape, but I knew I had best seem cooperative and throw the old folks off their guard. I got up, washed and participated in a game of ring-toss outside the Community trailer. Sarah was now delighted that our stay was indefinitely extended. She avoided me completely, occupying herself with one or another of the old people who seemed totally willing to do whatever she wished.

Later in the afternoon, an old man came into the Community trailer in his pajamas—he had obviously been taking a nap, a common habit among Settlement Tomorrow citizens. In his hand he held a wizened little organ with two small shriveled testicles attached. "It's happened, it's happened," he chortled gleefully. "It's come off—it's come off. Hurrah, hurrah, tonight the penis fairy comes to my trailer. Hurrah, hurrah," he waltzed around kissing everyone in sight.

"What does this mean?" I asked.

"What is it, what happened?"

"Oh, dear," said one, "she doesn't know."

"You'll have to tell her, Ida," said another.

"What? What? What is going on?"

Ida took me back to our trailer, and we sat down together for a talk about the facts of life—the birds and bees and all. "This is the way it went," she said, trying to be calm, educational, neutral, the way one is passing on sexual information to those not yet initiated. "After a certain age the important organs like the penis, the breast, the vagina, shrivel up. They—no longer needed, no longer given the proper fluids—they dry up, and eventually, as you saw with Harry today, they fall off. Here at Settlement Tomorrow we consider this an important occasion like a birthday or something. We put a little monetary surprise under the pillow of the person. The penis fairy, we call it just for fun, comes and rewards each loser with a little gift."

I protested, I never ever had heard of such a thing, it seemed unnatural, peculiar, disgusting. I was doubting—"Why, if that's true," I asked Ida, "why has no one ever told me about it before?"

She laughed easily. "Well," she said, "there really is a right age to learn everything, and if you had not stumbled into this community you probably would not have heard about this till you reached your seventies."

"But I can't believe it," I said.

"Look," she explained, "when you were three years old, you didn't know about menstruation. No one would have told, but it was going on all around you, all the time—you were just excluded from that knowledge on the basis of your tender years. Well, this is the same. Thirty-five is just too young for such things. You see how upset you are. It's because you're really too young to fully comprehend or understand it. You probably have peculiar fantasies. It's a shame—you should really not learn this sort of thing too young."

An incredible nightmare! "What else don't I know—what else is kept secret?" I asked.

"Now, now," she clucked at me, spoke soothingly. "All in good time. You'll grow old too and learn everything there is to know, just like the rest of us."

"Please, please, tell me now," I begged.

She chuckled and cooed. "Such an impatient little thing," she said and left the trailer.

God, how I desperately wanted to get out of there, but they sat always five or six around the telephone. I had to find some other way. There were other cars around. They were used to go into town, buy supplies, etc. I looked in them, the keys were gone. All right then. The thing to do was to steal the keys . . . Once I went into my grandmother's pocketbook and stole ten dollars to pay Bert Greenburg a bet I had lost. I had said I could run faster than he could, and it turned out I was wrong. Mrs. Greenburg found the ten dollars in Bert's pants and returned it to my grandmother, and there was a lot of weeping and wailing in the house, and my grandmother took me on the subway to Brooklyn to my mother's grave and made me apologize.

But now this was a matter of life or a kind of death, so I walked into the Community trailer and announced I was going for a walk in the desert. "I want to be alone for a while."

"Sure," said several old thin voices, scratchy like old records, birdlike.

I walked out of the trailer circle toward the sand that

stretched flat as far as the eye could see. Then I circled back toward the settlement. I looked in the window of a trailer—a man's underwear hung on a clothesline outside; inside there was the usual plastic furniture, and pictures of Rita Hayworth, Betty Grable and Jackie Kennedy hung above the small sink. Maybe in one of the drawers there was a car key—the damn trailer had to get pulled here somehow. I looked carefully around and saw no one, so I entered the little trailer door. By now I was so used to entering and exiting that I knew just when and how far to stoop. Once inside, I wanted to search quickly and get out. Guilt, fear, made my heart pound and my hands shake as I opened the first little drawer I saw. Good luck, the pot at the end of the rainbow! I saw some keys; they looked like car keys. I would take them, and at night when everyone was sleeping, I would try them on each car till at last a motor would turn and I could get Sarah and flee. I put my hand in the drawer. I heard steps, cackling. I jumped back. There was Mr. James Reid with two friends, Barry and Gordon.

"Whatever you were doing, it was no good, no good at all," shouted Barry.

"Bad, bad girl," said Gordon, his knees knocking against each other, as he shook his cane in my face.

"Girlie, that's not allowed," Mr. James Reid drawled.

"All right, I'm sorry. I'll leave, right now."

"It's not that easy. You came in, now you gotta play strip with us—you gotta take every little thing you got on right off." He smiled in a friendly kind of way. "We're going to play Doctor and you're the patient."

"I don't want to play," I said. "I refuse to play."

"Well, that's not such a good idea," said Mr. James Reid,

moving toward me. A shaky old man, I could probably push him over, but one of his friends was brandishing a cane, the other one had gotten a kitchen knife out of a drawer.

"Whoopee," he was saying, slashing at the air.

"All right, then, just step back and I'll strip." I took off my shirt and my bra, and let them whistle and shout awhile.

"Come on," begged Gordon, "a little touch."

I thought of screaming for help, but I didn't know whether I would get anyone to come and whether what came wouldn't be worse than what was already there. I was quiet, like a mouse that hopes the snake will overshoot his mark. Suddenly I heard steps. Ida came through the door.

"We were looking for you," she said to me, crossly. Turning to the men, she complained, "You were to follow her, that's all—just let us know what she was doing." To me she said, "It's not nice to provoke and tease old men. I had thought you were better brought up than that. Go back to my trailer, and stay there till I get you." She was really angry, and I felt guilty: guilty of trying to escape, guilty of bad acts, bad thoughts—Bad!

Four days went by. Sarah was enjoying herself. Her companions were building her a doll's house. She was always cutting or sewing or conferring with one or another of the old people. She had learned all their names and was even willing to allow them to call her by the names of their children or grandchildren. I was growing more and more frantic by the moment—one, two or three of them trailed me about wherever I went. The doctor came in a little black Volkswagen and set up clinic in the Community trailer.

While he was there, I was locked into the furthest trailer, which was pulled by a car (someone, at least, had a working car!) way out into the desert, so screaming would have been useless. I sat in the hot trailer all afternoon, randomly reading the movie magazines that had thoughtfully been provided. I was not ready to give up. I no longer felt sorry for the old people because their progeny had deserted them. I thought of nothing but how I could arrange to do the same.

On the morning of the fifth day, I found Sarah, sewing a velvet dress for her porcelain doll, sitting on the trailer steps alone.

"Sarah," I said, "don't you want to go back to school, play with children, see Susan and Blaine and Kingsley?"

"Oh yes," she said.

"Look, we can't leave here unless you help me get us out."

"I like it here," she said; mother-enemy, her eyes told me, don't push me around.

"All right," I said, "but when I ask you to do something, do it! Or else we'll be here forever."

"Okay," she said, her face serious. Did she understand or not?

At last, around four o'clock, I heard the sound of a car on the road. It was a plumbing truck. Cesspool trouble out here again. The plumber and his assistant got out of the truck, carrying a bag of tools. Most of the community went to watch him examining the cesspool. He lifted a cement slab and the smell became unbearable. The old folks backed off a bit, milled around watching the plumber take out his tools. Five of the men were escorting me to Ida's trailer where I would be kept till the plumber left. I was in despair; the morning stretched ahead of me like so much dead time. Suddenly the old man named Gary turned a strange purple color. He clutched at his heart, his eyes rolled back in his head, and he fell on the ground writhing. The others rushed to their stricken companion. One ran to get the oxygen mask and tank, another started artificial respiration; one ran to tell the group, and another was kneeling by his friend's feet. I stood there wanting to do something, but not knowing what to do. As the old folks started streaming away from the plumber and over to the man gasping on the ground, I saw my opportunity. Slowly, inconspicuously, I walked over to the plumber.

I tapped him on the shoulder. "Listen," I said, "your truck's blocking my car. If you give me your keys, I'll move it for you."

"Sure, lady, sure." The plumber was concentrating on his job. His assistant was still pulling on the cement slab.

"Sarah," I said, "get into the plumber's truck."

"But, mother, my doll, my porcelain doll."

The old folks realized I had the truck keys. They tried to block my way, but now I was desperate. I grabbed Sarah and shoved and pushed. My youth, my anger, served me well. I bit an arm that was placed in front of me. I kicked an old lady in the shins. I snarled at another man, pulling at the cane that supported him. "Sarah," I screamed, "get in." She did as she was told. I got the key in the ignition —realized it was a shift car. I hadn't driven one for years. I started it—stalled it—started again—managed to shift to first. The plumber realized something was wrong and came running. I shifted again into second and drove away in Leo's green truck.

Behind me I could see the old people running. I could hear Sarah crying softly. I saw them raise their hands, helpless to stop me, shouting and yelling. I saw tears on some of their faces—this loss was a repeat for them of other, more serious losses, but for me, a joy surged through my blood. The truck bounced up a hill. I had left everything behind, traveler's checks, papers for my divorce case, clothes—but I didn't care—not till kingdom come, not till the Premier of Israel addresses the Egyptian congress, will I return to Settlement Tomorrow . . .

Sarah said, "I really want my doll."

"Sorry, darling, someday I'll get you another."

"Someday, someday. I never get anything," she whined, but I was too happy to care. With each mile, the nightmare receded, and I felt safer than I had for many weeks. After all, I had just forced my own way to freedom, and I had never known before that I could force anything.

I took Leo's truck to town. I found a garage, and explained that Leo was working on the cesspool at Settlement Tomorrow and had lent me the truck to get help for my broken-down station wagon which was waiting near the entrance of the Settlement. Why didn't I call for assistance, the garage mechanic looked at me suspiciously. I smiled at him sweetly.

"We thought we'd look at some of the countryside around here."

It made sense enough—I gave him twenty dollars to go get my car and bring it back to town. I knew I would have a large bill then to pay for fixing the motor and the tires. I hoped I had enough cash. I had traveler's checks in the suitcases I had abandoned. I wondered if I could somehow get those back.

The money was Alex's money, not mine—I was an economic parasite living off the funds of another. Alex had enough. It didn't hurt him to pay me, to support me for the rest of his life—but I winced each time a check came. I was now providing no service in return for my bread and butter and felt like a union stagehand sitting around with nothing to do, collecting from the hard-working others just because the contract said so. I wanted to take his money and stuff it down his throat, the way you forcefeed a goose till his liver is enlarged and pulpy and he can no longer move his wings from side to side. But then what could I do? Waitress, receptionist, a little old for those jobs—I never did get that teaching certificate my grandmother had planned on. Now I could only sell lingerie in a department store, or maybe I could take a typing course, and who knows what might happen? The unexpected, the unpredictable, love again, this time better—unlikely but not impossible—I rose to the bait of my own thoughts. Maybe as I took a sharp curve on the road the car would sideswipe an approaching horse-van, and out would step a recently widowed oil tycoon who showed Arabian horses as a hobby, and we would strike up a conversation and then a friendship, and one day I might see to it that Alex's paintings were placed in the dusty lower basement of the museums of Houston and Dallas.

We hung around the garage waiting for the car. Sarah had four Cokes and complained of the heat, of having nothing to do, of losing her porcelain doll she had liked so much. We played a game of counting the cars that went by. We picked a color—I was green, and she was red, and the first to see ten cars of their color won. Nobody bought green cars in this part of Texas, and so I kept losing. We had an ice cream stick from a machine that ate up three quarters before delivering its fifteen-cent merchandise. Big wide fat flies settled on our arms and legs the minute we stopped moving, so we walked up and down the roadside. At last the garage attendant returned in my car with Leo and Leo's assistant.

"You didn't have to steal my truck, lady. I'd 'a taken you into town if you'd asked. Crazy New Yorkers" (he'd noticed the license plates), he shook his head, ". . . stripped my gears, I bet'cha," he sneered at me.

The wagon was in fine working order. The tires were in shape.

"Nothing wrong with the wires now, Miss," said the garage man. "They were all right when I got there," and he looked at me strangely.

I didn't care. I jumped into the front seat; Sarah climbed into the back. Our suitcases had miraculously returned.

"Look, mother," Sarah shouted, "the porcelain doll is on the back seat."

"I guess they're not such bad people after all," I said with a shiver.

"Could we stop on the way back and thank them?" Sarah asked.

"No, I don't think so," I said, pushing the motor up to 70 mph, anxious now to get out of the area entirely.

WE RODE ON for another 150 miles, crossing into New Mexico, stopped at a motel outside of Clovis. Sarah sent a post card to her father. I took a long shower, washing out the dust and heat. I looked at my body in the mirror—not perfect, not young, but not yet old—currents still ran up and down, and perhaps there was time for an ideal mating. Would you like to dance?—yes, I would, thank you.—What would you like to dance? Anything, anything at all.

The next day we started out again. Sarah was remote, lying on her back staring at the gray sky that threatened a summer storm. I had never been west before, never so far from the Bronx, which seemed exotic out here, like Hong Kong or Peking, teeming with unscrutable people rushing about buying and selling, children playing in the spaces between hanging laundry and moving vehicles. New Mexico seemed deserted except for an occasional rushing car, a truck, billboards advertising chewing gum and after-shave lotion.

It's hard to think of Jews in the desert forty years, wandering about with herds of sheep, camping out—all the Jews I knew hated animals, found their dirt disgusting and their heads dumb. My grandfather wouldn't even take me to the zoo—too boring, he said. My grandmother was afraid of cats. They can't do you any good, she'd say—look at the sharp little teeth and the nasty claws. I couldn't imagine anyone I had known as a child surviving in the desert at all. Maybe it was time to go back—start all over again—perhaps we needed a different set of commandments. The first ten had hardly produced a moral world. Why did God only light a bush? Why had He not cremated all of the guards at Auschwitz—Why destroy Sodom and Gomorrah, and leave Berlin a flourishing metropolis? Why did God stop Abraham from sacrificing Isaac, only to murder his progeny again and again? Sarah, were you overjoyed to see Abraham come down the mountain with your son in good health, or were you beyond caring, senile, wetting your robes, laughing at girlhood memories?

New Mexico had been beyond imagining in New York, and here it actually was, great red stones rising in the sandy distance, and long empty highways bisecting two vacant halves of a disc. It seemed as if the sun were closer, burning hot, yellowing all it touched. It seemed as if the rocks had been around when the pterodactyls crawled the earth, as if I had traveled so far to come to the beginning of time when men with odd jaws and long hair on their arms fought strange beasts in duels that were indeed honorable, honest and necessary.

The desert stretched out like the plains of Canaan where the Jews had camped, building little settlements, settlements always threatened by inner decay, a turning from the strict God to the looser ways of the neighbors, and threatened by war and piracy from the organized pagan tribes who also laid claim to the land and enjoyed a little pillage now and then. As we drove, a rage boiled inside of me—one Jewish girl from the Bronx divorced by an artist-fellow does not a diaspora make. And yet I seethed. I felt like Deborah, wise prophet, judge of sin, moral conscience of her time. I wanted to call a military man to my side: Kill, kill, I would intone in his ear, like Deborah promising Barak victory for Israel. Take the troops and sweep down on the Canaanites and end the oppression of Israel (for a while) . . . "Oh," says Barak, "I would never have the courage for such a battle, if you don't come with me." (Because she was a prophet, or because she was a woman? Or both?) . . . He was an incomplete warrior without her, and so the good Lord sent a thunderstorm, and the enemy chariots floundered in the mud, and easily Barak routed the hordes led by Sisera, who, poor man, sought safety in the tent of a friend whose wife drove a nail through his temple while he slept.—Why? Did that Jill hate her husband, hate all men? Or had she always desired to drive a nail through someone's temple and found that the fleeing general offered an opportunity? Deborah, an angry prophet, calling for the death of the enemy; Jill, whose own little slippered feet must have been stained by the blood that flowed from Sisera's wound . . . How many small Jewish girls have been called Debby and Jill—"Debby, set the table," "Jill, bring the candles,"—and behind the little ruffled dresses, the party shoes, the flour-stained little fingers, the hands that push doll carriages and string beads rest the genes of Deborah.—"Awake, Awake, Deborah"—and Jill. Down goes the spike into the soft and vulnerable skull. And I am a Jewish woman so without tribe, so without clan, that I doubt if I ever will find a home, that my exile will ever end. Such a peculiar lineage, to be a Jewish woman—some humorless prophets, others wily murderesses, most invisible to God, unwanted by God, subjected to men, and yet sometimes strong like weeds and mongrel pups, surviving everything, like a clever bacillus that alters itself slightly to defeat man's chemical brews. I am a woman anyhow whose history is long if not happy, and who therefore can expect a future.

I look at Sarah lying on her back, watching the clouds make shapes in the sky. Every now and then she sees something and calls out to me: "An elephant, there to your left; a dog, above you . . ." I try to look, but if I glance at the sky for more than a second, the car will go off the road, so

I always miss her shapes; sometimes I pretend to see them to keep the conversation between us going.

Meanwhile my anger focuses down to Alex, to his canvas stretched across the studio, the smell of turpentine on his hands as he searches around beneath my sweater for the nipples that have momentarily distracted him. I want him to want me, but not when he wants everyone else—not when I am an alternative, a handy piece that happens to be near. I am a romantic, I want to be loved exclusively. I dare to demand total devotion, the kind I am ready to give, and Alex laughs at such an idea, takes his hand out of my sweater. He wants an exciting bonfire around which a multitude of human forms parade and cavort, and I want a quiet cave, a candle, a secret worship that goes on forever. Clearly I am going to be alone in my cave, and that makes me shiver with cold. No eternal lights in the temple —that was all a myth—no oil mysteriously provided by the Lord. I am without.

The closer we get to Mexico, the clearer comes the realization I am divorcing the man who dazzled me, the love I could not keep because I am not enough for a man who requires a Rubens body, an Ingres face, a da Vinci smile, a Raphael skin, and a brain with all the skills of a Machiavelli to keep him interested. Well, damn him to hell, to eternal loneliness and bitter regrets; I'm going someplace new.

I was driving fast, when suddenly I heard a sound of a gun, a blast, beneath me. The car shook, shimmied. I lost control. I pressed the brake. The car skidded sideways. Sarah screamed as she was thrown against the side. I didn't see my life unfold before my eyes. I didn't think any last-minute thoughts. I was just overwhelmed with fear, like an animal facing the hunter's gun or a rabbit in the headlights' glare. We stopped. Sarah was all right. I was all right. The car was listing to one side. I started the motor—that was all right. I got out. We had a flat tire on the front right wheel—the old folks had replaced the tires with less than first-rate quality. I had a spare. I had a jack, but I really didn't know how to fix it myself. I took out the jack, a mysterious implement needing a man's abilities. I dropped it back into the car—another generation of women might be able to change tires, having learned like their brothers at some early age, but I was born too late for that new liberty. I needed help. The sky was darker than when we had started out. I would have preferred to be in a town, near people—not the only target for lightning for miles around. We rested like a beached whale on the side of the road and waited for a car to come by. I took a red sweater from my suitcase to wave for help. Twenty minutes (that seemed like an hour, time, too, having stopped turning with the wheels of our car) went by. A truck whizzed by—the driver was going about 80 mph and so didn't see or choose to see my sweater waving in the air. Another thirty minutes went by—the road was empty—it started to rain. Sarah complained of hunger, of boredom, of missing the early afternoon TV shows. A loud clap of thunder made me close the door—shelter was the least I could provide for myself and Sarah. The rain came down in torrents. I heard a car motor, but by the time I leapt out into the road to wave my sweater, the taillights were already disappearing up the road. We waited silently till finally the rain stopped. The thunder rumbled in the distance.

At last I heard a car in the distance. I jumped out onto

the road and waved my sweater. The car, a red Volkswagen, slowed, and as I breathed a sigh of relief, it stopped. The door opened, and out came a little man, so small at first I thought he was a young boy.

"What's the matter, lady, can I help you?" His chivalrous tone warmed me immediately and more than made up for his small size.

I pointed to the tire. I smiled my helplessness at him.

"Where you-all from?" he said as he started to roll up his shirtsleeves to go to work.

"New York."

"Well, I'll be a hog's hoof . . ." He stared at me and Sarah, who had climbed out to survey our rescuer. "I say, you-all aren't Communists are you? I know your home town is splitting its seams with commies, pinkos and atheists . . ."

"No, no," I reassured him, "we're not at all involved in politics."

"I am," he replied, sticking his chest forward. "I am a member of the National Riflery Association, New Mexico branch, a'course. We keep in training, target practice, hunting; we ain't gonna let God's beautiful country be taken by commies. We gonna fight to the last dying man."

"Who?" I asked. "Who's fighting?"

"My buddies and I. You know what I did last week? I wouldn't tell an ordinary lady, but I guess a New Yorker is all right—we drove us down across the border to this tattoo parlor where the soldiers all go, and I had put on my butt, one on each side, an American flag; whenever I sit down now, my country rests first."

He smiled at me, and I smiled back. One really can't be choosy on an empty road down the middle of New Mexico

He took my spare out of the car; as he lifted it, he staggered under its weight, and I felt guilty for imposing all this on him.

"Where are you going?" I asked him, as he heaved the tire down around the front wheel.

"My sister's invited me to dinner—she's an airline stewardess, and she's got a girl for me to meet. Says this one is perfect, and I got a hunch tonight's my night to make it big. I'll get married to her, and we'll get kids, and she'll cook my dinner. My sister says this one's such a honey, I can hardly wait till I get to El Paso. We're double-dating —my sister's got a pilot boyfriend, a giant man. She always has gone for size, that one has . . . but she told me when she called me last Wednesday that this friend of hers was just a bittie bird—that's why the airlines only let her fly the South American route."

"Do you own a gun?" asked Sarah, bluntly.

"I sure enough do—it's a long rifle with a powerful sight and I'm an A-1 shot. Last winter I got a trophy." He was unscrewing the hubcap and finally the punctured tire fell over on its side. "First step's done, ma'am," he said. He brought the spare up to position and fitted it on.

The jack had lifted the car's nose up . . . I had been strapped down on the table, my knees up and tied, when the doctor had said, "Push, Push, I see the head." And I had thought, I won't push, I won't do anything you tell me at all. I'll keep my baby inside. I won't start this division. I'll hold it in. The doctor said "Push, Push," the nurses pressed on my abdomen, they injected something into my strapped-down arm, and I fell blank into the dark and then they took her out of me. And when later I held her in my arms and felt like the crisp early mornings in the mountains, like green and moisture and sunlight, like a landscape of valleys and hills that stretch forever, I couldn't understand why I hadn't wanted to let the baby be born, to let the doctor take her. How had he become my enemy at just that moment? Maybe it was being strapped in that had turned me nasty . . . The little man was fitting the spare tire into place. Sarah walked over to his car and peeked in the window.

"He *does* have a gun, Mommy; look, a really big gun."

He turned around to tell her, "You're not allowed to touch that unless you've been trained." As he turned, his shoulder must have hit the jack, and the car lurched from its awkward position and released the fender from its pinchers, and it fell forward. The jack turned over on his foot. He screamed and hobbled a few steps. I rushed over to him. He sat down.

"God damn fucking foot, God damn fucking Good Samaritan—God damn women—can't do anything for themselves," and he writhed about on the gravel.

At last he calmed down some and allowed me to gingerly remove his boot and his sock. His foot was swelling before my eyes, and it was clear he couldn't walk or drive a car. He was very pale and perspiring over his upper lip. All I had for him was some Lifesavers in my purse. Sarah got them out, and he picked all through them till he came to an orange one, his favorite flavor, and then piled the others back in the package.

"Keep them," I said.

"Thanks." He put them in his pocket, wincing as he turned about.

I thought I could take his car into some town and get help, but he told me the nearest place was an hour away, and I couldn't leave him lying on the road embankment for two hours.

"Mother," said Sarah, "we should've flown—it's so much easier to get divorced if you fly. And I bet they serve good meals on the plane. What'll we do now?" she said.

"Don't worry," I replied, "a car will come soon and help us."

"I got a date in El Paso, I promised my sister I'd be there," the little fellow whined and growled. "It's a goddamn plot," he said. "Someone's screwing up my life."

"No," I tried to reassure him, "it was just an accident, could happen to anybody."

"New Yorkers," he squinted his eyes at me. "You sure you don't know any commies or commie symps? What's your name?" he asked suspiciously.

"Johnson. Emily and Sarah Johnson."

"Oh," he relaxed a little. "Any relation of Lyndon B's?"

"No," I said, "but don't worry, I'll take care you get to a doctor."

"Will you call my mother, too?" he said. "She runs a beauty parlor in Dallas. Ah, don't call her, she'll just yell at me for getting in trouble, for messing around."

"It was very sweet of you to stop and help," I told him. Was I a siren that wrecked men's ships, or a Circe that turned them into pigs, or was I the lonely Minotaur that longed to see the sunlight on the blue waves and was instead imprisoned in a dark labyrinth for crimes beyond his understanding?

"The pain's going up my leg, do you suppose they'll have to amputate?" Tears filled his eyes.

"Of course not," I said. "Haven't you broken anything before?" I asked.

"Well, when we was ten, I busted my arm when Henry and I stole Mr. Mayfair's watermelons—not stealing exactly, just taking a head home, you'd say."

"You'll be okay," I reassured him again and looked down the road for help.

No cars, no sounds, no birds, just the scrub landscape caught in the afternoon's shadows, bugs crawling around the stones. I went into our car and turned on the motor. I put the radio on to its loudest volume, letting the rock music erupt and fill the void, keeping each of us from thinking too much, or feeling too much. Sarah climbed into the station wagon and fell asleep, stretched out like a snake on a flat rock, thinking about shedding its skin. A truck zoomed past at 90 mph. It couldn't have slowed to help us if it had wanted to, but maybe the driver had seen us and would send someone else back to help. It was hard to tell how much time passed. The young man explained that he was a third-level sharpshooter, and that he hoped next year to make second level, but he needed more practice than his store-manager job allowed him time for. His foot was swollen and blue. I put my red sweater over it so that neither of us would have to look at it. "Goddamn way to spend Saturday," he snarled at me every now and then, and I agreed we were not good company for each other. I was dusty and dirty and needed a shower. I was hungry and thirsty; if no one ever came along, would I shoot the young man that had stopped to help us and eat him for survival's sake, or would that be beyond my moral possibilities? Of course I wouldn't know till I was tested. He looked extremely unappetizing right now.

I heard the sound of horses' hooves on pavement. I could hardly believe it—a wagon gaily painted in red, blue and purple, with flowers and leaves decorating the driver's seat—two horses with bells on their harnesses pulling the wagon along—behind them another wagon and a third. I thought first it was a circus, or an advertisement for some nearby store, but as they drew closer, I could see the men and women sitting on the wagon's seats—dark, dressed in shiny velvets and satins. They had to be gypsies. Gypsies in New Mexico—I laughed. Maybe they would tell my future.—Maybe my future would hold wonders—was a dark handsome stranger waiting around the corner for me? Was my lifetime going to stretch on forever? "Look, Sarah," I woke her up, I called her out of the car, "real gypsies." Groggy, she was still excited by the horses, shiny black aristocratic-looking beasts. I waved my sweater—the first wagon stopped, the second wagon stopped, the third pulled by my side. Sarah patted the horses. The gypsies climbed down. "My tire," I explained. "I don't know how to fix it—I'll pay you if you'd help. This young man has hurt his foot trying to help me. He needs medical care."

I would have preferred to be rescued by a car, but a horse was better than nothing. "He's thirsty, too; he probably's broken his foot," I talked on. The gypsies stared at me coldly.

"Listen, Mrs. Johnson, don't trust those gypsies. Don't let 'em near you. We've had experiences. Come here, Come here." I bent down to my wounded hero who whispered, "They're thieves, every damn one of them is a thief. Get me my gun out of mah car. I'll take care of it."

"Now, don't panic," I said. "You don't need your gun."

The southwest is full of bigotry. Like botulism in a soup can, the whole system's poisoned by suspicion and hate and narrowness. Violence leads to violence. I wouldn't give the redneck his gun under any circumstances . . . and instead I patted him affectionately on the back. No need for antagonism or the cold shoulder. Besides, who knows how long before another car or truck comes this way?

"Those gypsies stole my mother's radio, and my sister said her friend saw a gypsy putting a curse on her chickens and they were all eaten by wild dogs the very next night," my broken-footed rescuer called out in a rage.

But I paid no attention to him. The gypsies had gathered about my car, looking at the tire and the jack, and one or two of the ladies had climbed in and were opening our suitcases—overfamiliar, compulsive, unable to control their curiosity, but not alarming. The children had gathered around Sarah who was asking them all about the horses. Several of the young men approached the red Volkswagen, but my friend called out from his reclining position, "Get away from there, or I'll kill you." The gypsies smiled sweetly at him; in a display of white teeth they laughed good-naturedly and turned away from the car. So much for the menace of the gypsies, I thought. I saw the children pulling at Sarah to come with them into a wagon, and I wondered if I ought to stop her, keep her by my side; and then I despised myself for fears of the Third World, for suspicions like my broken-footed friend's, for fearing differences of skin color, when in fact my kin were the gypsies—wanderers, outsiders, stubborn, isolated persisters in a culture always alien to the countryside, always passing through, accused of crimes, persecuted, hounded and yet proud, secretly feeling superior. No wonder we rubbed shoulders on the way to the crematorium. Jews are just word-burdened gypsies.

I saw a glitter in the dark eyes of the lead lady. Her multicolored skirt swung on her hips, rustling with each step; her silver jewelry clanked together. Jews and gypsies together near the border to Texas! How marvelous—we survive and travel about, no matter who despises us, who tries to eradicate our particular color, our life style. If Darwin is right and it is the most fit that truly do survive, we, Jew and gypsy, are in magnificent condition.

Sarah climbed out of the wagon, carrying a carrot to give to a horse. I noticed several of the women talking to her, showing her their bracelets and earrings. A band of ragged children, babies, young ones, appeared, staring at us and the car, with wide silent eyes.

"My tire," I explained again to one of the men, "the jack has toppled over, but I'm sure it wouldn't take you long to complete the job. I don't quite know how to work it," I smiled apologetically.

An old lady sat wrapped in a crimson sheet on the top of the second wagon. She had a transistor radio by her side, and it blared rock music from Station WVEO of Fort Worth into the countryside. It was not the banjo and tambourine I had expected, but I was still pleased to meet real gypsies. They talked awhile among themselves as if I weren't there.

"I'll pay good money, whatever you people think is fair," I called out.

My friend with the broken foot called me over. "Look," he said, "just get my gun. You're a nice lady, get me my gun." He started to crawl on his belly to his car. I hated to see him hurting himself. The pavement was obviously causing him pain.

"Look," I said, "just rest here and if there's any trouble at all, I promise you I'll bring your gun right over to you."

"All right," he agreed. "You sure you don't have any commie friends in New York?" He squinted at me as if the truth of my political affiliations could be revealed in my skin tone, my creases, the circles under my eyes.

No one had taken up my offer of money to fix the tire. The male gypsies were leaning against the wagons laughing and talking with each other—I began to feel curiously excluded and nervous. One of the young men did a headstand on the roof of my car. The girls all whistled and clapped their approval. I wanted one of them to fix my tire, and fast. I had now lost all my anthropological, sociological curiosity and wanted only to be on my way. I jumped into my car and began to honk my horn. The sound blasted out. The horses started, some bucked; the gypsies all turned around to look at me. Now, I thought, I'll get my tire fixed.

I got out of the car. "Money," I shouted, "money to anyone who fixes this tire."

Sarah came rushing over to me—"Can I have my ears pierced, can I please have my ears pierced? Nerita will do it for me right now and give me gold earrings too!"

"Miss Lennitt's girls do not have their ears pierced at ten," I said, rather stiffly.

"But Mother, please," she said.

"This is no time," I shouted at her, "to bother me with earrings. We have to get this tire fixed, don't you understand?"

Sarah looked at me, shocked; why was I so angry at her? Her face closed away from me.

"Get me my gun—I'll get 'em to fix it with a bullet in their backs," shouted my friend.

"I told you," I said quietly, control coming back to me at the mention of gun, "I told you I'd get you your gun when and if we need it."

No one moved. I noticed they were all watching Sarah who was now standing quietly by my side. One lady went up and felt her body, her rib cage, her arms. "Open your mouth," she instructed Sarah, who was so startled she did as she was told. "Good teeth—clean," she reported; "Good!" They all talked some more. I thought they were deciding whether or not to take my money and fix my tire. There was a threatening silence. They went up to the old woman and whispered with her.

Suddenly, before I realized what was happening, they all jumped back onto their wagons. The drivers took the reins of the horses. Two young men in yellow silk shirts and gleaming white teeth appeared by my side with a purple quilt. "We like your daughter, Madam. She will be happy with us"—and instantly they covered her head with the quilt, picked her up, screaming and kicking, and threw her onto the back of one of the wagons, jumped on, and the horses galloped off. It happened so fast I was numbed. Then I ran to the red Volkswagen, and in the back seat I saw the well-loved rifle. I grabbed it out and ran back to my friend who had turned on his belly in shooting position, but the wagons were already up the field.

"Shoot the horses, not the drivers," I yelled at him, my faith in his marksmanship perfect.

His face grew taut, he sighted, he pulled the trigger;

his body recoiled a little with the force of the gun. He shot again and again.—I expected to see the horses drop, to see a wounded gypsy fall to the ground, but in fact, untouched, the wagons moved on out of sight.

"Goddamn—shit—goddamn—shit!" My friend beat his fists on the ground. "I just haven't had any experience with real moving targets—a few rabbits, a pole cat, that's all. You got me my gun too late. It's all your fault, I should 'a shot them right away, as soon as they stopped, goddamn gypsies." And on and on he railed into the empty sky. I sat down beside him, unbelieving, uncomprehending. It seemed impossible, but Sarah was truly gone. The road was empty. For the first time I was truly alone with myself.

I WAS STUNNED, of course—frightened, helpless, sitting on the ground beside my car, I held my knees close to my chest and rocked myself back and forth, comforting my pain the way I held Sarah when she was a baby, warm, sweet, clinging onto my shoulders. What was I going to make of her, a person like myself, an educated soul who sat a distance away from all other people, loveless, unadmired, angry, bitter, disappointed? If she grew like me, reflected me in her behavior, if she had my culture . . . oh, poor child, it would be so sad. If I could choose for her, I would select a whole new set of options, another culture, another way of being; a Tahitian native, a Polynesian girl with a red flower in her dark hair—something that wasn't cramped, that could sing, make love, have great sex in many beds. Maybe a gypsy with gold earrings, slipping through the borders at night, taking whatever's needed; maybe, I held my knees close, Sarah would be a happy gypsy. She would not have to run away from me in five or six years, never writing, hating the memory of me, a divorced lady with all my peculiar whims; she wouldn't have to despise me daily or learn ways of cutting me, embarrassed silences before her friends, whispering on the telephone secrets she hopes I won't hear.

Did she still need me at ten, did she want me to love her, or was it already at the end of its function, the mother-child thing? . . . Should I not be free too, begin alone, Lot's wife, a pillar of salt? Perhaps it was better for Lot's wife that way, alone in the desert, not responsible for anyone else, just standing still watching the earth turn on its axis. Perhaps the gypsy theft was a kind act of fate, freeing me to flee to Tierra del Fuego; perhaps there I'll find an Indian fisherman who'd place me in his shack, and we would have babies that spoke a strange native tongue and loved the sea, running each evening down the sand, bare-assed, to greet their father pulling in his small boat. And so my mind wandered, as I sat there till evening musing over so many possibilities.

God had thought it honorable of Lot to give to the screaming citizens of Sodom his daughters to rape rather than hand over the male strangers who had come to his house and sought hospitality. With such a peculiar code of honor, it's no wonder that Jews have met such a bad end. Maybe Sarah would be a great gypsy, singing ancient songs to her babies born by campfire, surrounded by friends, never isolated, never behind a door waiting for a telephone to ring.

At last, toward evening, a car came down the highway. As I heard the motor, I rushed into the middle of the road, swinging my red sweater. The car slowed as it saw me and stopped. A man got out. Thank God, a man, and not a young girl or another woman. He was a traveling salesman for drip coffee pots. He was professionally always kind and helpful, and the habit had become his soul. "Oh my, oh my," he moaned over the young man's broken foot. He gave him a shot of whiskey he had in his glove compartment. He fixed my tire in five minutes, helped me lift the young man into my car and promised to stop by my motel in El Paso to find out how everything was. He accepted no money, extracted an emotional pledge to never again buy any kind of coffee pot that didn't drip, and off we all went.

It turned out we were only an hour from El Paso. "I'll take you to a doctor," I told my friend. "Tell me where to go."

"Now that's nice of you," he said, "but I think we better first stop at the police and get them after your daughter, ma'am." I thought of Sarah riding on a wagon out into the desert—was she frightened, or did she feel exhilarated? No longer was her life predictable, small and mean. Now she was cut loose from expectations of the new math, history papers on "Life Along the Nile" and a future with a thousand choices, none of them promising joy—Here she was, riding in a wagon, part of an ancient tribe, a true changeling child.

I insisted on dropping my friend off at his sister's motel. "My God," she said when she saw him, "what's the use of trying to fix you up with anybody, you're always such a mess." I gave him his gun to use as a crutch and he hobbled out of sight.

I took the car to my motel, checked in, lay down on the bed. Sarah, Sarah, do you want me to come for you, or do you want me to go on my way? The thought crossed my mind to leave her—impossible, but possible. Let her be her own person. Let her find her own way, gypsy or not. Cut the cords; like an animal, refuse responsibility past the first infantile moments. I would be without her, sparse, clean like a bone. Tomorrow would be mine to devour alone. I didn't need her like an albatross around my neck —See, see what sin that mother has been into—I didn't need her cold eyes saying, "It's a cheat," "It's a lie," "I don't believe you." I didn't want ever again to hear the thumping of the ball and the rain of jacks on my car floor. I didn't want to know that I had recreated my own failings in another, to watch her pick a man who would use her badly. I didn't want to live it again through her. I had enough to do holding myself together.

The idea gathered force. Leave her be, and drive on down to Honduras and swim naked in the tropical waters, pick pineapples and bananas, and listen to the rain falling on the palm leaves.

I would write Miss Linnett's School a letter. "Sarah will not be returning next fall due to unusual circumstances—if possible, please refund my tuition deposit." I would write her father. "Dear Alex, I have lost Sarah, just now or years ago, I'm not sure. Nothing about our marriage was a good idea, nothing we created together can survive our disunion. You may reduce my alimony proportionately, since I no longer have a child to take care of."

I lay on the bed a long time thinking about Sarah. I looked out the small window of the motel room that overlooked the parking lot. It was dark. Sarah would be sitting around a campfire with the gypsies. Stunned, frightened, somehow she would be waiting for me, expecting me to return for her. If I didn't come, if the night turned into night and I didn't come . . . I felt an anguish open in me, hers and mine commingled—a terrible black pit of love and need and caring, an iron maiden into which we were both forced. I sat up. What if she'd been raped, or harmed, hungry or cold, murdered or teased? . . . I quickly dialed the police. The sheriff's car appeared moments later at my motel door.

I told him the entire story, and he radioed for more police cars, for helicopters, and said as he put my sweater around my shoulders, "Don't worry, ma'am, heard this often before. Pesty gypsies—don't really harm anyone, but drive us all crazy with their carryings on. Why didn't you come directly to the police?" he asked.

"Blacked out. Stunned," I explained.

The helicopters landed in the motel parking lot. I got into one with the sheriff. Six other planes hovered in the sky. We rose in the air. The noise of the propellers made me feel as if I were inside a sanitation truck where the garbage is ground to nothing. The vertical rise and the open windows frightened me. Icarus was a male, not a female—a female would have waited for a boat to rescue her. In the dark the helicopter's searchlights scanned the ground. The scrub bushes looked like black dots on the sand.

"Don't worry," shouted the sheriff into my ear, "we know where those gypsies tend to hide. We've chased 'em often enough before."

Again I was sitting beside the Gestapo, the authority; why were my enemies and friends so confused? The landscape below seemed lifeless—no houses, no animals—like the moonscapes, a country unsculptured by life. I grew cold and tired. Perhaps the gypsies had at last learned how to avoid the large noisy copters, had hidden beneath the ground in some subterranean kingdom where outcasts, like earthworms, could multiply in peace.

"Goddamn gypsies," the police pilot was shouting to be heard above the wind, when suddenly over on our left we saw a cluster of flames, small blinking lights like Christmas bulbs on a terrace of a high-rise housing project. As we abruptly came lower, my ears stopped up and bubbled painfully. We saw horses and wagons, saw the gypsies rushing around packing up, trying to avoid the police. The copters landed like big-bellied Trojan horses; out came the police, surrounding the campsite.

"Stay back," shouted the sheriff.

"Wait here," yelled his second-in-command; but now I was frantic to find Sarah; I kicked off my shoes so I could run faster and followed the police.

When I reached the wagons, I saw the faces of the children hiding between the wheels, their eyes wide with terror as the sheriff spoke through his bullhorn, and guns were pulled by about twenty police.

"Men and women, up against the wagons, hands raised."

I could see the sullen look, the heat of anger in the gypsy faces. I could see the police frisking them for weapons, hands unnecessarily rough, contemptuous.

"Sarah," I screamed and screamed, running from wagon to wagon. The flashlights of one of the policemen followed me around.

Then, from under one of the wagons, in among a group of children, Sarah cried out, "Here. Here I am, Mommy, here I am."

Had they harmed her? Was she raped? Murdered? Or just frightened? Then I saw her. I ran. She ran to me.

"Mother, I thought you'd never come. I was so afraid I'd never see you again," and she cried and cried with relief, with the memory of fear, and I cried with the closeness I felt, her arms around me, our bodies touching, my need for her, hers for me. We were one piece of flesh with different movements, but united.

"Sarah, I'm so sorry," I said. "I'm so sorry—were you hurt?"

"No, no," she quickly reassured me. "I had my ears pierced. Look . . ." and there were two gold earrings running through new and slightly swollen holes in her ear lobes.

"You look," I said, "like a gypsy," and she hugged me again, my daughter, my soul, my one love.

Sarah enjoyed the helicopter ride back to the motel. "Look at the town," she shouted as we approached El Paso. "Like a toy village, like a witch doctor shrank everything, it's beautiful up here." I hugged her. She was alive.

No, I wouldn't press charges. I had to go to Juarez, and then on, I explained. "Well, we'll lock 'em up, anyway—and then chase 'em away." The sheriff understood my need to get on. "Hope you get a new man soon," he said, tipping his hat politely. And the police cars rode off into the Texas night.

Sarah and I slept soundly, untroubled by the loud whir of the faulty air conditioner, or the trucks and buses going past on the road.

In the morning we started on the last lap of the trip. Would we fly home, abandoning the car, would we travel on down to Panama, to Nicaragua? I would decide later. After the divorce, what kind of future, what shape would it take? I was too old to feel like a budding flower, like an open book; like a daisy on a chain, I had wilted. But as we drove the few miles to the border, I thought of the new man the sheriff had wished for me. I wanted a gentle man like my grandfather, a dreamer of good dreams, but a man who came home to dinner, who took me to Italian restaurants and Saturday night movies, who talked about his work with me, who spoke a shorthand we learned to share in which our view of people and events quickly could become common matter between us. I thought of a man whose body excited me, wildly at first, and then again and again through the years, when he would lean over suddenly to touch me, to rub a thigh, to find a hand, to reach out in the dark for a closeness of body, a part in part; of shared trivia—of bills to be paid, travel plans made, the dog walked, the slip covers sent to the cleaner, the plants watered—a closeness of body part in part, a man whom I loved even when he had a cold or boils or picked up a hookworm in the Caribbean; a man who loved me, wanted me even when I was menstruating and had to use a towel to protect the sheets, or if I had pink eye or fatigue, or hated myself, or burned the dinner, or lost my pocketbook, or my suspected skin cancer turned out to be an infected hangnail. I wanted a man whose mind I found interesting night after night. Before the Late Show was over, we could talk and think and constantly grieve together over the state of things we could not change and change the things we could. Such a man, such a love, such a middle-class vision!

Who knows what new illusion I am in danger of selling myself! . . .

At the border, uniformed Mexican police were making token checks of the identification and baggage of foreigners—Americans. They were pretending that there was something illegal you could bring into Mexico that wasn't already there.

When it was my turn, the guard leaned into the car. "Listen, lady, you want to buy some dirty pictures—the real thing—make you so happy." He smirked at me.

I noticed the gun on his hip, felt he might make trouble for me if I didn't buy his dirty things. "How much?"

"Two dollar," he said. I gave him the money and received a cylindrical package wrapped in brown paper.

I drove the short distance to Juarez. When I could see the pink church steeple over the hill and knew the Mexican lawyer would be seeing me within the hour, I stopped the car in a shady spot by the side of the winding road. There was a picnic table provided by the state for tourists, and I got out, sat on the wooden bench and tore off the brown wrapper. Mexican whores, I thought, kissing soldiers—a large brown breast rubbing against a high brown penis—so I anticipated my pictures. I pulled some paper out of the cardboard cylinder. It was a cheap tourist copy of the Declaration of Independence 1776, signed by John Hancock *et al.* I had been cheated again.